Dear Re[...]

I may ha[...]
always b[...]

My drea[...] [...]y
came true when I accepted a newspaper job on
a New York daily. I had my coveted NYC address
and 212 area code.

I loved the sounds of the city, even when sirens
woke me in the middle of the night. It didn't
take long for me to discover the secrets of the
subway system, which I knew better than how
to get around my neighborhood. And I finally
stopped counting the number of Playbills in
my closet, all proof that I'd been to Broadway.

Despite the grumbling you hear from many
New Yorkers, who love to complain about
congested streets, crowded subways, the high
cost of living and the ten-dollar hamburger, trust
me, they wouldn't dream of living anywhere else.

How could I not set a romantic comedy story in
the city I love above all others? New York is the
perfect secondary character—majestic parks,
quaint neighborhoods and eccentric residents.
The city and romance are made for each other!

So I have to tell you, it *was* a difficult decision
for me to leave New York for Arizona after almost
five years, and almost as difficult saying goodbye
to Megan and Jack in *She Said, He Said*. Now
here are two native New Yorkers who have a very
interesting story to tell, so I'm going to let them
have their say....

Happy reading!

*Cheryl Kushner*

# "Don't you think we'd both be better off if we talked about it? Resolved it?"

Megan glared at me. "I don't want to get involved with you, Jack. Not that way. We get together and just clash and it's exhausting and I can't take it anymore. I'm not going to cry my eyes out over you ever again."

I knew all about the exhausting bit.

Wait. She just admitted she'd cried over me.

"We need to keep it...professional," she said with a bit of a hitch in her voice that told me that perhaps Megan wasn't as sure about this as she wanted to sound. "The apartment renovation comes first. That's business."

"What about our friendship?"

She shook her head.

"We're not friends?" Now I was confused. "I've known you forever. Why aren't we friends? What happened?"

"We had sex."

# Cheryl Kushner

## She Said, He Said

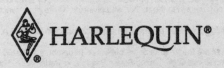

# HARLEQUIN®

TORONTO • NEW YORK • LONDON
AMSTERDAM • PARIS • SYDNEY • HAMBURG
STOCKHOLM • ATHENS • TOKYO • MILAN • MADRID
PRAGUE • WARSAW • BUDAPEST • AUCKLAND

ISBN 0-373-44205-X

SHE SAID, HE SAID

This edition published by arrangement with Harlequin Books S.A.

® and TM are trademarks of the publisher. Trademarks indicated with
® are registered in the United States Patent and Trademark Office, the
Canadian Trade Marks Office and in other countries.

www.eHarlequin.com

Printed in U.S.A.

## ABOUT THE AUTHOR

Cheryl Kushner trained as a journalist and is an award-winning writer and editor who has worked for several major newspapers in a variety of jobs—including news reporter, features writer and entertainment editor. After almost five years in Manhattan and living through some, but not all, of her heroine Megan's experiences, Cheryl moved to Arizona, where she's now the features editor at the *East Valley Tribune*. An avid romance and mystery reader, Cheryl has been writing fiction since 1993 and was first published in 1998. *She Said, He Said* is her first Flipside novel, but she's hard at work on another romantic comedy with a chick-lit twist that's also set in Manhattan. She loves to hear from readers. You can e-mail her at CherRW@aol.com

## Books by Cheryl Kushner

SILHOUETTE ROMANCE
1659—HE'S STILL THE ONE

For Bonnie, Claire, Connie, Emilie, Leigh and Mary
Friends Forever

# 1

---

*Megan*

SINGLE LIFE LESSON #1: Sometime between the onset of puberty and the day you discover that new AAA batteries won't restart your biological clock, you will make a Big Mistake.

The good news is that just when you think the Big M (as I've come to call him) isn't ever going to take a hike, he's outta here and the memory begins to fade, thankfully.

And life rambles on.

If you're lucky, all you're left with is a slight cringe whenever you see him or hear his name.

Today was not my lucky day.

My Big Mistake (cringe here) was standing at the northwest corner of Ninety-third and Broadway on Manhattan's Upper West Side, wearing wrinkled tan chinos, beat-up tennis shoes without socks and an aqua T-shirt that screamed in red letters, Caution! Bad Boy At Work.

He looked slightly rumpled. His dark wavy brown hair was neatly mussed, just like it would be if some woman had:

a) run her fingers through it, or
b) just shoved him out of bed.

Considering the Bad Boy-Big Mistake in question was current TV heartthrob Jack Spencer, the answer was more than likely:

c) both of the above.

And now, as he did every Monday night at ten o'clock on national TV, Jack looked much too sexy for words. At least, words I could utter on a public street without causing a riot or being arrested.

For a brief moment, I considered crawling back into the taxi and pleading with the driver to take me as far away from Manhattan as fifty dollars and some loose change could get me.

Which meant I'd end up:

a) in northern New Jersey,
b) on the far side of Queens, or,
c) staying right here, fifty bucks richer, and toughing it out.

None of those choices was the least bit appealing. However, I had no choice, because Chloe Farrell, my new business partner, had slammed the cab door shut and was pulling me across the street, her eye on you know who, mindless of cars, buses and trucks shooting by at speeds guaranteed to maim.

"Megan Elizabeth Sullivan," she hissed in my ear, "you didn't tell me."

No, I hadn't. But there was a very good reason—even if I wasn't planning to share it in my lifetime. "He isn't supposed to be here."

"You said we were going to look at an apartment you used to live in. For a client," Chloe responded with a touch of pique in her voice. "You *didn't* say that client was one of America's newest 'sexiest men alive.'"

Actually, one of America's newest "sexiest men alive" who *used* to be my best friend.

Considering the longtime friendship between the Sullivan and Spencer families, it had been a miracle I hadn't run into Jack in the nearly six months since he'd become my Big Mistake.

I sucked in a deep breath. "*I* can do this. I *can* do this. I can *do* this. I can do *this*."

I tried not to stare at Jack, who'd lowered his sunglasses onto the tip of his patrician-like nose and looked straight at me with those see-everything dark green eyes, as though challenging me to take those final steps.

And I don't mean steps across the street. I mean steps that might let him wiggle back into my life.

Which wasn't going to happen. No way. Never.

Since traffic wasn't slowing down, and since I had plans today that did not include a visit to the E.R., I needed to get across the street as quickly as possible, and in one piece.

So I repeated the four little words one more time, giving each equal emphasis—"*I can do this!*"—and sprinted.

A task I wouldn't recommend if you're wearing nearly four-inch heels. (A tribute to Manolo Blahniks, which I love but can't afford.)

But then I was *there*. I'd made it. I stood on the sidewalk, in front of the man with whom I'd spent a long night indulging in mind-blowing sex. On the rooftop of the very same Manhattan brownstone apartment that Chloe and I were here to look at.

To be accurate, mind-blowing pity sex.

Pity sex. I'll never forgive myself.

Or him.

"Can you say hello?" Jack smiled as though he hadn't a care in the world—or a memory of the night I couldn't forget, mainly because I dreamed about it constantly.

The swine.

"You're not supposed to be here."

He looked somewhat taken aback. "Where am I supposed to be? You want to look at my apartment, don't you?"

I didn't. Not really. But a promise was a promise. Even one made under extreme duress and sealed with maternal guilt. Still, I hadn't been sure that I could keep this one, despite Chloe's support. But then I'd heard it from an obviously not-too-reliable source (Jack's mother) that he would be working all day down at the Chelsea studios where his TV show, *The D.A. Chronicles*, was filmed.

So the scene uptown was supposedly Jack-safe and Jack-free.

But here I was, with Chloe, because even though I might not want to work for and/or with Jack Spencer, Chloe and I couldn't afford to lose a whopping big commission on a challenging renovation project on the Upper West Side.

I'd recently quit my job with one of the city's top interior design firms *and* signed my life away for the next thirty years on a small-business loan in order to open Design Time with Chloe. Not only did I have myself to support, there was the extremely demanding feline who shared my life.

"Of course we want to look at the apartment," Chloe said, finally, and introduced herself. "And, of course, I'm one of your biggest fans." She extended her hand and Jack accepted it, a bit warily. What did he think Chloe was going to do? Rip it off as a souvenir and offer it for auction on eBay?

After some pumping motion, the handshake should have ended, but Chloe hung on as though she wasn't ever going to let go.

I nudged her shoulder. "Enough."

Chloe silently slipped her hand from Jack's and offered him her ten-thousand-dollar smile, courtesy of her orthodontist.

Jack returned it with a wide smile—dimpled, of course—courtesy of Mother Nature.

I tried very hard not to clench my teeth, for fear of upsetting all the dental work that had cost me as much as a year of college at the Rhode Island School of Design.

Jack's gaze focused on me instead of the blond-haired, blue-eyed, size zero Chloe, who usually sent men panting to their knees. I would have been impressed, except that I knew I was the one woman he could resist.

Aside from that one night when we'd both lost our minds.

Here's a one-word description of me: cute.

I'm a New York City native. I'm five feet six inches, blessed (or cursed) with flaming red hair that refuses to be tamed and freckles (enough said about that).

My moss-green eyes war daily with my daily-wear contact lenses, and my curves are shaped in a capital *S* expanded, rather than a lowercase *s* compressed. The only way I'm ever gonna see a size zero on the label of the clothes hanging in my miniscule closet is when it comes after a one. Right now we're at one-two.

I'm smart. People seem to like me. While I'm not a ballbuster, I am armed with definite opinions and am not afraid of letting the world know them.

Jack took a step closer. "You're looking good, Meg."

I'd like to think so. I'd spent a good portion of what had been my weekly salary on this outfit—a cream-colored linen skirt that hit me a good two inches above the knee, matching tailored jacket ribbed in black and a sleeveless peach silk camisole with a neckline curved in a rounded *V*.

Oh, yes, and those four-inch knockoff Manolos, which made my feet hurt like hell and made me almost as tall as Jack. As long as I didn't wobble, I'd be okay.

Still, considering it was nearly ninety degrees in the

middle of an unexpected late May heat wave, and I could feel the sweat beading on my forehead and down into my cleavage, I tended to believe he was speaking pro forma.

Jack wrapped an arm companionably around my shoulder and eased me westward, in the direction of the brownstone. I willed myself not to react when I felt a shiver race up and down my spine, and reminded myself what had happened the last time he'd touched me.

Since it would be terrible professional politics to slap his arm away, I didn't. We needed this job.

Jack didn't, I should note here, wrap his other arm around Chloe's shoulder, but she sidled next to him anyway. The three of us made our way toward 352 West Ninety-third Street, which happened to be:

a) my childhood home,
b) the building that Jack was going to move into,
c) a place that desperately cried out for interior renovation (according to my mother and Jack's, the co-conspirators here), and
d) the scene of the crime, aka the scene of my Big Mistake.

We made our way to the strictly decorative wrought-iron gate spanning the stone entryway. Now that Jack was up there, popularity-wise, with a certain sexy rock star who lived just around the corner, I imagined screaming girls/young women/not-so-young women/gay guys pushing and shoving through that lockless gate in order to pay homage to their virile hero.

What I wouldn't give to be a fly on the wall when the co-op board heard all the noise and met the Jack Spencer Fan Club.

"You grew up here?" Chloe whispered in delight.

The building resembled a castle from a fairy tale, with turrets, beveled glass windows and wrought-iron trimmings. When I was a child, I'd pretended I was the princess and Jack was the prince who'd come to save me from the evil queen.

I didn't share any of those memories with Chloe. Instead, I nodded. "Long before it became an overpriced gotta-have-it location for overpaid, overachieving yuppies." Each apartment contained in this little oasis would sell today for close to a million bucks. Before any renovation.

A good many longtime Manhattanites (case in point, my entire family) have, over the past decade, fled the city for the suburbs, which, they soon found out, were no more affordable.

The trade-offs for green land were lawnmowers, gas-guzzling SUVs to cart the kids to play dates, exorbitant property taxes and a bitch of a commute to the city.

"I'll never understand why your parents migrated to New Jersey," Chloe said, "when they had this." She waved her hands in the direction of quaint Riverside Park, a quiet little retreat a few hundred feet up and east of the West Side Highway.

Neither did I. But my parents had chosen suburbia over the city, and sold apartment 6-B in this six-story building to the Spencers—who already owned 6-A—sometime during the ceremony that marked my high school graduation.

By the time I had left for college, my parents called the rolling hillsides of Montclair, New Jersey, home. Whenever I got back to the city during school breaks, I'd stay at the Spencers' in what had been my old bedroom. I liked to think my parents understood.

Now I had the opportunity of a lifetime to remake the

space that had once been two separate apartments into something lasting and wonderful.

Just as soon as Jack signed on the dotted line of the contract. Which was a foregone conclusion because, well, after meeting our mothers, you'd understand that neither of us had much of a choice.

Just as we were about to enter the elevator, Chloe's cell phone rang. She checked the number, offered an apologetic smile. "Sorry. Have to take this. Meet ya up there."

And so the elevator doors closed, leaving me and Jack Spencer alone, slowly moving upward in a metal box that felt claustrophobic. And hot.

"I meant it, Meg. You are looking well."

Hmm. From "good" to "well."

"Been a long time."

It's been four months, three weeks, two days and—I looked at my watch—fifteen hours since we did It.

"I've tried to call you."

Don't do me any favors.

"Aren't you going to contribute to this conversation?"

No.

"Would it help if I said it never should have happened?"

I don't know about you, but I haven't met any woman who would be thrilled to hear a guy she had great sex with apologize for the sex.

Before I was forced into even more conversation without saying a word, the elevator jolted to a stop, the doors swooshed open and I pushed out into the hallway, keeping as much of my pride intact as I could. Even as I felt Jack's gaze bore into my back like a laser beam.

He breezed past me, fitted a brass key into the old-fashioned lock, opened the door to the apartment and ushered me in.

Dark, heavy curtains framed the windows. Spanish-style furniture packed the huge room. All the hardwood floors needed sanding and refinishing. The best way to describe the art on the walls was to call it "flea-market chic" courtesy of the seventies—not my favorite decade for decorating smart or savvy.

"Except for a recent paint job, it looks the same as it did when they moved in thirty years ago," Jack said, as though reading my mind about the cream-colored walls. "And we can't forget the two kitchens."

Ah, yes, the two kitchens.

A short history, personal and otherwise, follows.

1. My parents moved into 6-B the day they married, and there raised the three of us (Patty, Ellyn and me, in order of arrival) until they moved across the Hudson River.

2. Once the apartment was sold, the Spencers promptly knocked out the connecting wall and—presto!—they had a bigger living room, and three and a half bedrooms (the half bedroom being an architectural anomaly). Plus, of course, two baths and two kitchens—both kitchens have all the original appliances.

3. After years of talking about it, Jack's parents were soon moving to Fort Lauderdale. They sold this apartment to Jack for one dollar. He then bought them a spiffy, brand new two-bedroom condo with wall-to-wall gray carpet and white walls, and a view of the Atlantic Ocean.

Jack's mother, who was recovering from breast cancer surgery, got happy tears in her eyes whenever she talked about moving into her new home. Until then, they were living here and Jack remained at his tiny apartment in Chelsea.

4. The Spencers did nothing to decorate the side of the apartment that had been 6-B, other than shuffle oversized

furniture into it, so this space was a new homeowner's nightmare and a designer's dream.

5. I shared my first *real* girl-boy kiss on the rooftop of this building when I was sixteen. With guess who. We were just practicing, which was good, because the experiment left us laughing so hard we almost rolled off the roof.

Back to the present. I'd barely had time to reminisce about the apartment before I was greeted by a growl, followed by a series of loud barks that belonged to a monster the size of a baby elephant.

"Good puppy," Jack said fondly, and grabbed its collar so it wouldn't lunge. "Good Achilles."

Achilles? Stay tuned for Jack's warped sense of humor.

"Puppy? Did you say 'puppy'?" I stared at the Great Dane, who came up to my waist, and, you'll recall, I was wearing four-inch heels. "How old is it, anyway?"

"He's eight months." Jack rubbed Achilles behind the ears. The, er, puppy, smiled up at him adoringly. To each his own.

"We've got a problem," I said, keeping my eye on Achilles, who was drooling, also adoringly, all over Jack's chinos. "Dogs and renovation projects don't mix. Especially big dogs. And big renovation projects. You'll have to keep him away from here."

"He's a puppy," Jack said with exaggerated patience.

Right. "Like an SUV is really a sports car. How do you control him, anyway?"

Jack snapped his fingers. "Achilles, heel!"

I groaned.

But the puppy, without hesitation, moved to Jack's side. And then flopped onto his back for a belly rub. "I thought you'd understand how important it is to be adopted by a pet."

Of course I did.

My sisters and I had grown up with a series of kittens that had become cats, my latest being Emma, a silver tabby Maine coon who followed me like a heat-seeking missile all over my studio apartment in Greenwich Village.

Jack's mother, however, had barely tolerated the goldfish and the turtles he invariably brought home following our treks through the city's weekend street fairs. As a child, Jack had bonded with his pets only to see them die, die, die.

At one point my mother had felt so sorry about Jack's lack of pets that she'd allowed him to keep a pair of white mice in our apartment. That was, until the day they got out of their cage and moved next door to live with the Spencers. Enter mousetraps. End of mice as pets.

The Achilles situation, I decided on the spur of the moment, was the perfect excuse for me *not* to take this job if I couldn't deal with the inevitable roller coaster of emotions about Jack that I'd be riding throughout the project.

"Look," Jack said, "he won't be a problem."

"You're going to take him to work and write him into the show?" Sometimes sarcasm became me.

Jack rolled his eyes. I think Achilles did, too. "I'll find some dog sitter to…sit. Not here," he added hastily. "There's gotta be someone willing to take him during the day."

"That's a start. But what about after hours? It makes no sense for you to move in here while the renovation is going on. Why don't you stay at your place in Chelsea until the project's done?"

"That's not up for discussion." The firmness in his voice brooked no argument.

"You're going to be spending a lot of money—yes, Jack, a lot—on this project, no matter who designs it for you. I'd hate to think of twelve-hour days of hard labor wiped out every evening with one swipe of that dog's tongue."

"I'll deal with Achilles." Jack's clipped tone, the tactic his TV character used when pinning a witness to the stand right before the final commercial break, didn't scare me.

"You do that." I broke eye contact and started my walk-through of the apartment, searching for a neutral space, preferably one without memories. Fat chance.

Three large rectangular windows overlooked Riverside Drive to the west, while three to the north offered a view of Ninety-third Street. Two identical fireplaces dominated the north wall, followed by another three rectangular windows.

Framed pictures cluttered both mantels.

But only one picture mattered at the moment.

My hand shook as I reached for it. "I thought your parents had moved their personal stuff to Florida."

"The way they're going about it, they'll be shipping stuff back and forth for months. But what needs to be gone will be gone before the renovation begins. Anyway, there's some stuff here I might want to keep."

"Stuff like this?" I indicated the baby picture in a sterling silver frame.

Not just any baby picture.

A five-by-seven full-color photo of two toddlers, lying on their stomachs on a pink cotton blanket in the middle of Riverside Park, naked as the day they were born.

Me and Jack Spencer.

Could this day get any worse? In a word, yes.

I thrust the photo in Jack's face. "I can't believe you're displaying this."

He grabbed the picture, turned it face down on the mantel.

I reached for it. His hand tried to slap mine away. And hit air instead.

"Is this the only way you want to see me? Naked? Even when I'm dressed? You, you…jerk. Swine. I can't even think of the appropriate word to describe you."

He scrubbed his hands down his face. "Megan, it's a baby picture that's almost as old as we are. Don't you think you're overreacting a little bit?"

Yes I was. I knew that. But everything about my being here felt wrong, wrong, wrong.

Was I heading for another helping of my Big Mistake?

I gazed up at Jack and fixed a look on my face I hoped was fierce and unyielding. I must have succeeded because he wisely took a step back. Then another.

"I see you naked even when you're dressed?" He shook his head in amusement. "That's a good one."

I reached for the dog leash draped across the back of the sofa. "If you don't want this wrapped around your neck, take yourself and Achilles for a long walk so I can go through this mausoleum and see how much it's going to cost you to push it into the twenty-first century."

Jack took the leash, and Achilles—true to his name— heeled. "I'd hate to think we've lost our sense of humor about some things."

I pointed at the door. "Go, Jack."

He went, and just managed to avoid bumping into Chloe, who stood in the doorway, a look of bewilderment mixed with fascination on her face. "I hope I'm not interrupting anything."

"Chloe," I said as calmly I could, "meet Achilles. He belongs to this heel here."

Jack's back stiffened but he didn't say a word. He shoved the puppy out the door and followed. A moment later, I heard the elevator doors swoosh open, then swoosh closed.

I slumped onto the windowsill. Okay, so I hadn't played fair. Maybe I was being a bit too bitchy. But then again, on New Year's Eve, Jack hadn't played fair, either.

Chloe nudged me over and sat. "It's time to tell all."

She was right. Maybe spilling it would help get my angst out in the open. "I don't know where to begin."

Chloe crossed her arms over her chest and waited. "How about this? You and Jack Spencer grew up together. And you are so sorry that in the three months we've been business partners you never mentioned him once, knowing that I am such a fan of *The D.A. Chronicles*. And then, you can admit he's the one."

I slowly turned to look at her. "I don't know what you're talking about."

"Sure you do. He's gotta be your Mr. New Year's Eve."

"Good guess." Although not a difficult one, since last Monday night I'd stopped by at Chloe's just in time for the opening credits of *The D.A. Chronicles*. I'd spent the next sixty minutes muttering at Jack's image on the TV screen and avoiding her questions about that not-so-normal reaction to TV's latest hunk.

I've learned that it's one thing for best friends to share a first kiss, but once you've done it, there's no going back to being just buddies. And there's no guarantee of going forward, either.

Some more history: A little more than a year ago, I met William Tyler Marshall III, aka Trey. Even before he proposed, just a month into our relationship, I'd decided he was the man with whom I'd share the perfect NYC life, complete with a Fifth Avenue town house overlooking Central Park.

I was madly in love (and lust).

Jack, however, who usually had a word or two (usually caustic) about the men I dated, was uncharacteristically quiet. He didn't even laugh, or crack a dimpled smile when I asked him to be my man of honor.

Which would have told me something if I'd been paying attention. But I was too busy planning my dream wedding with the help of a high-priced wedding planner who, now that I recall all the signs I was too besotted by love/lust to see then, was busy planning a wedding of her own.

My conversation with Jack, the morning after the night Trey proposed, went like this:

Me (waving my giant emerald-cut diamond in Jack's face): What do you think?

Jack: Does it matter what I think?

Me: You're supposed to be happy for me.

Jack: I want to be happy for you.

Me: It's important that you and Trey get along.

Jack: Why? You're marrying him. Not me.

Do you see a pattern here? It only got more depressing, so I'll skip to the end.

Me: I love him.

Jack: You love him now. But do you see yourself loving him five years from now?

Of course I did. No one goes into a marriage believing or hoping it will fail.

Me: Say you'll be my man of honor. I can't imagine walking down the aisle without you.

Jack (after a long beat): Or me without you.

After that conversation, I felt better. Much better. But looking back, I was the only one celebrating, because neither Jack nor my fiancé could spend more than a few minutes together in a room without one of them walking out.

(The Cold War between the two really heated up the moment after I officially announced my wedding attendants would be my sisters and Jack.)

My sisters and their husbands were pleasant but cool. My father frowned a lot. My mother was terminally teary-eyed whenever she talked about the wedding so it was difficult to tell what she really thought. Or felt.

And then, on Christmas Eve, a week before the wedding, I got this telegram from Trey, wishing me holiday tidings and oh, by the way, sweetheart, I've eloped to Vegas with our wedding planner. P.S. Happy New Year!

So much for his plans to spend his Christmas Day bachelor party in Vail, Colorado, carousing with his college buddies.

It was easier to call off a wedding than you might have thought. Once the shock waves subsided.

The day after Christmas, I canceled the church, the flowers and the cake, and placated the caterer when she should have been placating me. I insisted on calling almost four hundred guests myself.

Then, with my mother's help, I packed away my dream dress in the bowels of her attic and swore that, once I got my equilibrium back, I'd auction the dress on eBay. The dress was still packed away in that attic. But any day now...

Sure, at the time I was hurt, depressed and felt as though no one would ever love me. Through it all, however, my best friend Jack held my hand, comforted me, let me cry endlessly onto his shoulder and told me it was all for the best.

Easy for him to say.

I wandered through the next week as though I was living in a continuous bad dream. And then came New Year's Eve, which was supposed to have been my wedding day, and my honeymoon night.

While the rest of the world celebrated, I was deep into a full-scale depression.

"And I'd never felt so alone," I told Chloe, who'd listened to my tale of woe silently and attentively, "and so utterly lonely, in my life."

In the days leading up to what would have been my wedding day, I'd insisted to my family I needed to be by myself. But at eight o'clock on New Year's Eve, the time I was to have walked down the satin-covered aisle, I felt this urgent need to be with people I didn't know and who didn't know me.

People who wouldn't judge me and find me lacking the gene that made men fall in love—and stay in love—with me.

I put on my coat, gloves and scarf, and caught the subway up to Times Square. I wandered through the crowd for an hour or so, but there were too many happy people, far too many happy couples. And so I got back on the subway, rode up to Ninety-sixth Street and Broadway and found myself walking toward the old apartment on Ninety-third and Riverside.

The sky had darkened as much as it could, considering the glare of light that always hung over Manhattan. The snow fell lightly. It was quiet. And I felt at peace for the first time in months. The wrought-iron entry gate was open, so I parked myself on the stone steps and waited for the new year to begin.

But I could hear a party going on. I felt a tap on my arm, and some smiling stranger, who'd opened the door behind me, told me I'd be welcome.

All of a sudden I didn't want to be alone.

As I rode the elevator, I wondered what the hell I was doing. Why was I choosing to be with perfect strangers when I could have gone with Jack's parents to New Jersey and celebrated with my family? And for a second, I regretted that I'd declined when a few girlfriends had suggested they throw me an unwedding reception.

When the elevator doors opened on the sixth floor, I saw that the party had spilled out of the apartments and filled the hallways. Someone passed me a glass of champagne. I drank it greedily. Then another. Downed a third, too.

And then I saw Jack Spencer.

He looked as though he'd just stepped out of central casting. His rich brown hair was a little long, those sparkling green eyes bright with a bit too much bubbly. His red Henley shirt (the one I'd bought him for Christmas) was tucked into old, faded jeans that were worn in all the right places.

What was Jack doing alone on New Year's Eve?

"I don't know who was more surprised," I continued. "He smiled, came over, kissed my forehead and whispered, 'Glad you got my message. Too many people here. How about we escape to the roof?'"

There hadn't been any message as far as I knew, but that didn't matter. He was here. Just what I needed. I followed him up the short flight of stairs. He had a bottle of champagne in one hand, two glasses in the other. It had stopped snowing, and the roof was covered with a thin layer of white that was busy melting.

He kissed me again, on the lips. No, I kissed him. Whatever. We kissed each other deeply, with a frenzy I can't remember ever feeling before. Or since.

Suddenly, though, Jack put on the brakes. "Not here." Then released them. "Oh, what the hell. Here."

And we tore at our clothes, tossed them to the snowy rooftop and had sex, madly passionate monkey sex, in the same spot where he'd first kissed me when I was sixteen.

Most everything that happened after that is a still a blur.

The next morning, I woke up in a twin bed in what had been my old bedroom, wrapped around Jack Spencer, who was deftly playing the role of longtime lover.

He whispered in my ear, "I'm truly sorry, Megan."

Talk about breaking the spell.

Then his cell phone rang.

Jack leaped out of bed and took the call. In the hallway. So he could have privacy.

I scrambled into my damp, wrinkled clothes. Ran down five flights of stairs and over to Broadway. Hailed a cab home. Unplugged the phone and vowed that I'd never, ever, see or speak to Jack Spencer again.

Pity sex.

"He'd felt so sorry for me that he slept with me," I told Chloe. Tears clouded my eyes and I let them fall. "And ruined everything."

I gazed out the window. Jack Spencer, the man who used to be my best friend, who was now neither friend nor lover, leaned against the lamppost in front of the building. As though on cue, he looked up at me, those all-seeing eyes covered by sunglasses, his expression impossible to read from this distance.

Were some Big Mistakes, I wondered, destined to hang around forever?

# 2

*Jack*

I ALWAYS LIKED TO pretend. Which was probably why I chose to be an actor.

These days, I got paid lots of money to pretend to be a New York County (that's Manhattan) Assistant District Attorney with more guts than brains on *The D.A. Chronicles,* a top network crime show.

My press clips claimed I was the ideal macho tough guy. Six months ago, I was an actor constantly on the hunt for work.

*Not* an out-of-work actor.

You gotta understand, there's a big difference.

I've made more money in the past few months doing a regular TV role than in my entire professional acting career, which basically consisted of off-Broadway shows running more previews than actual performances. My notices were decent. The plays needed a lot of work.

Of course, I'd done small parts on TV. When you're an unknown, every résumé line counts, so there's not an actor in the city who hasn't had some kind of role on *The D.A. Chronicles.*

Over the past four TV seasons, I'd been a victim (a lingering close-up), friend of the victim (one line of dialogue), brother of the accused (no dialogue but a good minute of camera time in the courtroom) and an innocent bystander caught in the crossfire who chose vengeance over common sense (guest-starring role). The wonders of makeup, lighting and camera angles meant actors could do multiple roles.

I'd auditioned for other acting jobs I thought I'd be perfect for. But unfortunately for me, the directors didn't agree. I auditioned for jobs I didn't really want, but got and took, because I needed to pay the bills.

For a two-week stretch early last summer, I thought about quitting acting for good. But the puzzle of my professional life started fitting together last July. I was cast in what would be the fifth season premiere of *The D.A. Chronicles*, a two-parter where I got to play this hotshot lawyer who had everything, but who looked as though he was gonna take a powder because of the pressure.

But something unexpected happened during the filming. They liked *me*. I mean, they liked me as the character of Logan Hunter, rogue A.D.A. And the two-part episode led to another episode, then another that turned into a five-episode story arc. Hey, they kept throwing money at my agent and pages of dialogue at me, so it was easy to say yes.

Life seemed to be looking up. But then, the story line ended. Although there was some big talk about bringing back the character, nothing happened immediately. So I read for a few small TV roles. Didn't get 'em. It was Christmas. I was heading back toward being broke and having to consider alternatives, none of which I care to mention here.

A woman I'd been seeing over the previous few months—not seriously or steadily—decided she could no longer afford to live in Manhattan as a starving artist, and went home to live somewhere in upper Minnesota.

So I wasn't looking forward to the start of a new year.

I was dateless, jobless and without my best friend, Megan Sullivan, who had just avoided the biggest mistake of her life when the man she was going to marry proved my theory that he was, indeed, a world-class jerk.

At first, Megan had cried on my shoulder. But as it got closer to the non-wedding date, she was in such a funky mood that she refused to answer e-mails, v-mails or impromptu visits to her front door.

Then, on New Year's Eve, about an hour before midnight, right before my bleary, champagne-challenged eyes, Megan got off the elevator.

Her nose was red from the cold, a deeper red than the red curls that framed her face.

I loved her freckles.

I loved the way her nose crinkled when she laughed.

I loved the way she always smelled as though Mother Nature came to her first before giving spring to the rest of us.

I wanted her. I guess I'd always wanted her, but had never had the guts, or the smarts, to admit it until then. That night, I had to have her, no matter the consequences. And, considering the amount of champagne zooming through my system, I wasn't worried about there being any consequences because it seemed, at the time, that she wanted me, too.

Trust me, I didn't have to pretend the sex I had that night was the best sex of my life. I couldn't then, can't now, find the words to describe the experience. Only the feeling that I'd found everything.

Not that I had any idea then what to do with this new-found everything. Or how to keep this feeling going other than to make love with Megan again and again that night.

I'd never played that role before.

When I woke up on New Year's Day, Megan slept,

curled next to me. Just where she belonged. I wrapped my arms around her, determined never to let her go.

And then my cell phone rang.

It was "the call" from my agent with an offer we couldn't refuse. A four-year contract, six figures and a co-starring role on a top-rated network show. Within months I'd shot from guest star with a few good scenes to co-star with his name on the opening credits. All because another actor got a little greedy come contract renewal time, and the network bosses weren't in that jolly a holiday mood to accommodate him.

Goodbye to the unemployment line. Hello, twelve- to fourteen-hour days (and nights).

My life was an actor's dream come true.

A beautiful woman in my bed. Megan.

A great job on a top-rated drama filming in New York City. Not Hollywood, thank the acting gods.

I hung up the phone. Then turned to shout out my good news to my best friend, the one person who I knew, just knew, would understand and celebrate with me.

And she was gone.

Okay, so why did I keep that baby picture?

I had no idea.

IT WAS FOUR A.M. and I was wide awake. The rain beat a tattoo against the windows of my Chelsea studio apartment. My continual poking at life's current problems hadn't brought me any answers or much-needed sleep.

The phone, which I'd tossed under the bed last night, rang. No, it shrilled.

"Fetch," I ordered Achilles, who was parked on my feet. The puppy yawned and went back to feigning sleep.

I reached under the bed and retrieved the phone. It's obvious who's training who here. "'Lo."

"Good morning, Mr. Spencer," trilled a sexy voice that belonged to a seventy-five-year-old grandmother I knew had been hired just to taunt me. "This is your four o'clock wake-up call. You're due in wardrobe at six, makeup at six-thirty and on set at seven. Have a nice day."

Before I could respond, there was a click. I imagined Sexy Voice placing a big check mark after my name and then dialing up her next victim.

I currently was living on West Twenty-third Street, in a ground-floor studio apartment with less than five hundred square feet of usable living space. The advantages included the price—less than a thousand bucks a month with utilities—and the location, barely a block from the Diamond Production Studios where my show was filmed.

Since I didn't need the limo the studio provided to take its stars to work, I had plenty of time for my ten-minute hot-as-Hades shower. If I was in good form, I could trick the abused coffeepot into producing an extremely strong version of caffeine that would rumble through my system all day. Yeah, and walk the puppy, who had more stored-up energy than any utility company.

Without a doubt, I was pumped about moving back into my childhood home at Ninety-third and Riverside. Even though I did grasp the concept that it was gonna be months before the place is remotely livable, according to A Woman Who Knows.

But I was moving in anyway, the first weekend in June, even if I had to schlep from room to room while the reno-vating was going on. Okay, it made no sense, but that's the way it's gonna be. End of discussion.

My new roommate and I needed our space.

In the two months Achilles and I had lived together, I'd learned that he loved his morning runs. If I had to choose between him zooming around the apartment more than a dozen times following my wake-up call or me getting up to take him for a walk, I voted for the latter.

Our routine consisted of a race across the block to Eleventh Avenue, then up to the newsstand on Twenty-eighth Street for my newspaper fix. I usually bought all the city dailies to read during the constant set breaks because, despite what you might have heard, making a TV show was ninety percent waiting and ten percent acting.

Back to the newsstand. It still shocked me when I came face-to-face with my mug staring out from the covers of the celebrity mags framing the front of the tiny cubby hole, which also served as neighborhood gossip central. Louie, the newsstand guy, actually read all these stories, and thought he knew the real Jack Spencer. All because I was on a weekly TV drama.

I felt like shouting, "People, get a life!"

With Achilles fed, walked and surrounded by his mountain of toys, I could begin my day. On the walk to work, I did this morning chant where I told myself how lucky I was to have a job that earned enough dough to pay for the tons of puppy kibble Achilles inhaled daily.

And, over the past few weeks, I'd added a few lines begging for calm during what was bound to be an expensive apartment rehab, because even before Megan and Chloe saw the place yesterday, I knew that it needed tons of work.

On this morning, as I flashed my ID to the security guards at the studio entrance, I added a coda: Please let me behave if I run into Megan Sullivan today.

I made my way down the hallway to an alcove with a sign that announced in big, black, block letters, Principal Talent. That's me. Such a lucky SOB.

My dressing room inside wasn't much (twelve feet

square) but it was all mine. That included a full-length mirror, makeup table and chair, beat-up love seat, two brass lamps and a twelve-inch color TV that used to decorate my home living space. There, I'd upgraded to plasma. My new-job present to me.

Hidden underneath the pillows of my love seat were dog-eared copies of women's magazines—an eclectic collection of titles that included *Chic, Glamour, Cosmo, High Style, Elle, Redbook* and *Ladies' Home Journal*—which I'd reclaimed from the recycling bins.

During set breaks, Alicia, my makeup goddess, and Rachel, the costume czarina, huddled together over these things like chick mags were the Holy Grail to getting laid. Or something. So I decided to check them out for myself. I was getting quite an education. Bold, colorful headlines shouted out stuff like, "10 Things Men Tell Us They Want From Women," or "Sex, His Point of View." Or this, "Tough Guys vs. Nice Guys: Which Turns You On?"

In my continuing effort to understand women, I picked up my latest find and turned to page fifty-six (past the fashion ads and the beauty advice) and read that Tough Guys were strong, arrogant, sweep-you-off-your-feet-then-stomp-on-your-feelings kind of guys. The footprints took years to erase. You, of course, tried hard to reform them, but in the end they got their way (and you).

Nice Guys were also strong, sensitive, sweep-you-off-your-feet guys who might stomp on your feelings, but they did it with panache and humility, and you thanked them for the experience. You thought the world of these Nice Guys, but couldn't see them as HEA (that's happily-ever-after) material because you held out for the Tough Guys.

Like many twenty-first-century males (tough or nice—was there a reason a guy couldn't be both?), I didn't get it.

As I heard my name bellowed to report for makeup, I thought that maybe what women wanted was men who thought like women but behaved like men. A scary moment for all us XY chromosomes currently populating the planet.

Whatever happened to men thinking like men? Seriously. There's a reason for two sexes, and despite my XY chromosome makeup, my brain did not *always* reside below my belt.

I was working toward enlightenment.

Alicia and Rachel waited patiently for me, reading this month's copy of *GirlTalk*, the new, hot magazine with a standard celeb on its cover.

My gaze wandered over to the trash can. Good. They'd tossed the current issue of *Chic*. I hadn't finished reading last month's tome, which had promised in a giant cover blurb a step-by-step plan to win back the one you lost. At first glance, the tips seemed pointless to me. However, you never knew what gems might be buried in the few pages stuffed between all the makeup ads.

I managed to snag the mag just as Rachel tossed a dark blue three-piece suit (followed by white shirt and indescribable tie) at me with the order to "Wear this!"

"Did you make war, or peace?" asked Sam Davies, who filled the door frame of the makeup room. He played a homicide detective on the show.

"You mean with Megan? The battle's not over. So I could use some advice," I said. Sam loved to dispense advice. He'd recently stepped out of the closet and wasn't afraid to display the all-too-feminine sensibilities within his six-foot, hunky frame.

Despite Sam's sexual orientation, women all across the country considered him a "get" and his TV "Q Factor"— popularity quotient—was off the charts. He kept his athletic body fit, and that, along with what I've heard women say with a sigh were his "do-me-baby" blue eyes, made Sam a real babe magnet.

Sam was one of the good guys. We'd established our boundaries and kept to them. And because of that, I felt comfortable sharing with him the kind of stuff guys talked about. Women. Sex. Work. Sex. Women. Sex. Football. Sex. Women. And, of course, sex.

"Come up with some dramatic, romantic and emotional gesture that will show her she can't live without you," Sam said.

"That only works in Hollywood chick flicks," Alicia said without taking her eyes off the magazine article she'd continued to read. "And it's so far from reality, you need to travel at warp speed to get there."

"What have I been telling you?" I said to Sam. "Besides, it's how I *felt*. Not how I *feel now*. A Tough Guy can only take so much rejection before he takes to the road."

"Tough Guys," Alicia said to no one in particular, "are vulnerable, but refuse to show it."

"Tough Guys aren't all they're cracked up to be," Sam said sharply.

Alicia just shrugged, her eyes still glued to what she was reading.

I tried to reach for my wallet to get the piece of paper I'd stuffed in there yesterday afternoon, but my hand was slapped away by the wardrobe czarina, who was busy stripping me of my jeans. You quickly lose all inhibitions in a job like this.

The jeans hit the floor and Sam plucked my wallet from its pocket. The wrinkled, yellow paper was easy to locate. He scanned the note, frowned, then shook his head and rolled his eyes.

My reaction exactly.

"Maybe if you read it out loud it will make more sense," I suggested as Rachel began to dress me.

He did.

Jack.
The place needs help. Badly. Figure six months *minimum*. Can't even begin to estimate cost.

However, I suggest you try to keep your day job.

If you want to take the next step, give Chloe a call and she can interview you re: your design thoughts.

I assume you have some.

—M

P.S. This consultation is gratis. Because, if we work together, I'm going to take you to the financial cleaners.

"She's consistent," Sam said with a chuckle. "She's going to make that apartment a showcase, and your life a living hell."

Not exactly the advice I was hoping for. "I'd ask you to dig a little deeper into the message subtext, but I can tell you're not on my side." I struggled out of my sweatshirt and into my tailored button-down lawyer shirt, vest and suit jacket.

"There is no subtext."

"There has to be a subtext," I said. "Women are all about subtext."

"Well, here's my take. She's letting you know she doesn't really want the job. But she feels pressured and obligated to help you. If you disappeared off the face of the earth today, she'd miss the big commission, but not you."

Sam thrust the note back at me, but my hand was slapped away. The paper fluttered to the floor, and I was shoved none too gently in front of the full-length mirror.

"That about sums it up," I said. "We're both being pressured. But it's a good step one to the plan."

Sam cocked a brow. "Jack, you have no plan. Despite all your protesting, you have some cockamamie idea that if you stand in Megan Sullivan's path long enough, she's going to fall at your feet and confess that she loves only you."

"You've been on the phone with the two Ritas?" I asked dryly. The Ritas were our moms, best friends since the dawn of time. Two women who had delusions that one day they would be related by marriage—mine and Megan's.

"One night of good sex—" Sam said.

"Great sex," I interrupted.

He shrugged. "Good sex, great sex… One night together in the sack doesn't translate into, or define, a relationship. She's had years to choose you if you were her choice."

"So what's wrong with me?" I examined my reflection. It looked pretty okay to me for a guy who'd just hit thirty. Thick brown hair, which needed a bit of a trim. Green eyes. Which, according to my network bio, flashed. No flab, because I worked out daily, and since the camera generously added ten pounds, even at six feet those pounds would bloat me.

"You're prime," Sam said with a grin. "Just not her cut."

Yes, Megan had made it clear that there's no room for me in her I-have-it-all-I-don't-need-you life.

First, by falling in love with a man who broke their engagement by telegram and eloped with the wedding planner.

Then, by engaging in great sex with me and walking out before we could talk about us, past, present and future. But Megan didn't return my phone calls, and only visited my parents when she knew I wouldn't be around. I knew the two Ritas were waiting for an opportunity to meddle, so it came as no surprise when they decided the apartment needed a major renovation and that Megan was the only designer in New York who could do the job right. Okay, I may have been cursed with the XY chromosome package, but I eventually got the message.

"And so," I said, "I'm movin' on. With Sheli."

"If you say so," said Sam with a shake of his head that told me he didn't believe me.

Here's the deal: To add to all the confusion in my life, I'd met someone else.

Sheli Bradshaw, twenty-seven, a petite and sexy brunette, was a publicist with a major Hollywood studio. We were thrown together last February at one of those post-Oscar parties.

I'd been invited to be an Oscar presenter (Foreign Language Film, I guess because I spoke a foreign language—New Yorkese). Not that I'd ever made a Hollywood movie, but the network that aired *The D.A. Chronicles* had rights to the Oscar broadcast and was happily packing as many of its stars onto the show as it could.

Sheli and I hit it off. Our first date was the *Vanity Fair* party, the second right *after* the *VF* party. Since neither of us was SOP—seeing other people—there was no reason not to see as much of each other as we could in twenty-four hours.

Sure, I thought about having sex with Sheli. I was still thinking about it. My ego, which needed a little TLC after being roundly rejected by Megan (at the time I met Sheli, Megan hadn't spoken to me in two months), couldn't help but be taken with a woman who smiled at me and meant it. But I hesitated on the sex thing, I guess, because I was still smarting from Megan's rejection.

During Sheli's business trip to the East Coast a few weeks ago, she told me the studio was transferring her to the New

York office this summer. I was cautiously optimistic about this relationship progressing past the date-cute stages and into something that would include sex without guilt.

But I made what I now realize was a major error in male judgment.

I brought Sheli over to meet my parents.

My mother, who I adored, possessed the subtlety of a ton of bricks. Her claim to motherly fame was that she said more with a smile than any number of words could express.

After Mom welcomed Sheli—minus any smile—she offered to share the closely guarded family recipe for potato salad that she wouldn't even give to Rita 1. I didn't have a chance to react before Sheli did the unforgivable. She said, "No thanks," and added that she did not have a working relationship with a kitchen or the items found within.

The evening went downhill from there.

Sheli, however, told me my parents were charming, she'd had a great time and it was too bad they were moving to Florida just when she was coming to Manhattan.

It took about a week to charm my mother back into her warm smile mode, during which I agreed it was wise to take it slow with Sheli, and yes, I'd host an apartment tour for Megan. I can't remember just when I'd committed to hiring Megan's new design firm to re-create my home—without even seeing a sketch or hearing an idea.

Did I mention I'm an only child?

We tended to take direction without question.

So when Alicia pointed at me and then at her makeup chair, I obediently sat. She wrapped a white towel around my still tie-less neck, and began to transform me into someone whose "Q Factor" was quickly rising.

"Stop squinting!" she ordered. "The foundation will crack, and the camera will make you look as though you've been engaging in downtown debauchery all night at some cool meet market."

If only. "Can I have some aspirin?" I was about to pay for the lack of sleep and the endless thoughts about Megan. About Sheli. About the state of my life, love and otherwise.

Alicia sighed the sigh of the put-upon, but dug into her magic tray and came up with two aspirin. I swallowed them dry.

She and Rachel exchanged one of those women's looks, the kind that make men feel as though they've missed something important. But I wasn't worried. After all, I had all these chick mags to help me out.

Still, with Megan thoughts crowding the brain today, it was hard to keep my mind on my work. I got through my two courtroom scenes with the minimum number of takes and a sufficient number of close-ups to keep my "Q Factor" in play. I wasn't due back on set until four, when I would get to pretend some more, probably until midnight.

My plan was to walk Achilles over to the Spencer's Deli in Chelsea and check in with my dad, who was making a farewell visit to his employees.

But first things first, I needed to respond to Megan's cryptic note.

Not to Megan. She'd made that perfectly clear.

So I decided to call Chloe, who seemed to like me a little.

Like most New Yorkers, I was able to accomplish a dozen other things and talk on my cell at the same time. As I crossed the busy intersection at Twelfth Avenue, I punched out the number that I'd memorized.

Three rings and a click.

"Good afternoon. Design Time."

"Chloe..." I searched my memory. "Chloe Farrell, please."

"Who's this?"

The voice sounded suspiciously familiar. "Megan?"

"Jack." Significant pause. "Chloe's not here."

It sounded as though she was going to hang up. "I'm calling to talk about my design thoughts."

Long silence.

"Chloe's up in Westchester today. How about tomorrow—" there was the sound of turning pages "—at three?"

"Can't. I'm on set all day. How about later this afternoon?"

Another long silence.

"Chloe won't be back, and I can't. I have...I'm busy."

"Any time this weekend?" I mean, after all, how long would it take for someone to listen to my thoughts? From Megan's note, she believed I had none.

"We're closed."

Must be nice to be your own boss. "I have an hour free now."

"Now?"

"Megan," I said, as I wrestled the door to my apartment open and grabbed Achilles' collar before the puppy could sprint down the hallway, "take half an hour. Consider it a professional courtesy. Bill it to my account."

"Now is not good." (Translation: never is better.) "I'll have Chloe call you." Click.

"This doesn't bode well," I told Achilles, who barked in what I took for agreement. Or maybe in happiness, because he knew he was going on a walk.

And me? I needed a Spencer's cheesecake fix to sweeten my sour mood. Thank you, Megan.

If you'd ever visited Manhattan, chances were you'd stopped in at Spencer's Deli. There were three in the city:

Upper West Side, Chelsea and Times Square, the latter location where the number of people who waited for wedges of cheesecake was often longer than the line at the half-price theater ticket booth across the street.

There would be, if Martin Louis Spencer had his way, a fourth location, somewhere along the oceanfront of Fort Lauderdale. He reminded us daily that he had to do something with his free time when he wasn't playing golf. Trust me, my dad, who's in great shape and edging toward seventy, would never truly retire.

The opening of the first Spencer's, a few steps north of the subway station at Ninety-sixth and Broadway, coincided with my entry into this world. Just as Dad cut the ribbon, Mom went into labor.

She left for the hospital in a taxi. Dad followed as soon as he was sure the store could survive without him. Ten hours later, two Spencers became three, just as Dad walked into the delivery room.

With enough pastrami sandwiches and cheesecake to feed the entire maternity ward.

In my lean days, and in between auditions, I used to work the counter at the Times Square deli. I knew more about slicing rye bread, just how lean *lean* pastrami was supposed to be and the best way to make chocolate phosphates than any of my Jewish friends in the city. And I knew cheesecake.

But as the Nielsen ratings as my witness, my working-behind-the-counter days were over, even if *The D.A. Chronicles* got axed from the network schedule later today.

I stuck my head inside the store entry, waved, and then waited for my dad to come out.

He carried an iced bottle of root beer and a wedge of creamy blueberry wrapped in waxed paper. And some slices of lean pastrami for the puppy, who swallowed them in a gulp.

"So, you and Megan gonna be a team?" He took a pull on the bottle and then handed it to me. The man thought in sports metaphors, and found it easier to dispense advice that way.

"We're working on it."

"This is another brainchild of the two Ritas."

There were some things (like having sex with your mother's best friend's daughter) you didn't tell your parents. Especially when your parents and her parents have dreamed from the moment they placed Megan and me on that blanket in the park, naked, that one day the two best friends would be strolling through Riverside Park with their mutual first grandchild.

Time to change the subject.

"How's the rest of the packing going?" I asked.

Dad shrugged. "Your mother has it under control." What he didn't have to say was that she couldn't part with a single stick of furniture or piece of pottery and wanted to move it all to Florida but it wouldn't fit in the new condo. "So, you get the rental car?"

"I'll call later this afternoon. It's only Wednesday."

"They'll be gone. Your mother will never forgive me if she has to drag bags and boxes on the train all the way to New Jersey on Sunday, because you couldn't take the time, right now, to do this one easy thing for her."

For her, as in, not for him. Because my father would never ask anyone to do him a favor. But in my mother's name, that's another story. Like he couldn't call the car rental place the way he's done thousands of times before.

He pointed to the cell phone hanging from my waist. "Call now."

I sighed. Punched number three on my speed dial. Less than ten minutes later, we had a late model Ford something-or-other that would be waiting for us at exactly noon on Sunday.

My mission: drop them off in Montclair, New Jersey, at the home of the other Rita, where they'd spend the night before heading to Fort Lauderdale the next morning out of the Newark airport. I'd say hello to the Sullivans, then take the car back to the city.

And spend the rest of the day watching my plasma TV. Such was the life of a popular TV star.

I was going to miss my parents. I loved 'em. I enjoyed being around them, even when they were driving me nuts. I wanted what's best for them. My mother thought that was Florida. Since her cancer scare, Dad would have done anything for her. So would I. Well, almost anything.

She told me she'd come back to live in Manhattan part-time when I found a nice girl, got married and provided her with several grandchildren. And if she got to choose her daughter-in-law, her choice would be Megan Sullivan. No one else, in her opinion, was good enough for me. Especially not, as she put it, "this woman from L.A. who doesn't cook and appreciate family traditions. She doesn't have to be Jewish, but she should have more than a passing acquaintance with what goes on in a kitchen."

Neither Rita had cared for Megan's fiancé (actually, no one in either family thought much of him, but out of deference to Megan we accepted him, coolly). And while no one ever said aloud that the best thing to happen to Megan was for the engagement to be broken, no one wanted to see Megan hurt, either.

I know women believe men possess the sensitivity of a gnat (with the gnat probably one step up in the evolutionary scale), but men do have feelings, even if we mask 'em with macho.

Fact: Women want real heroes.

Fact: Men can't always live up to women's expectations. Or sometimes our own.

Which was why I was moving on. Why I was determined to find the perfect woman, eventually marry her and give my mother the grandchildren she'd been waiting for.

Would that woman be Sheli Bradshaw? I didn't know, but I was taking the time, and the trouble, to find out.

And I was coming to terms with the fact that when Megan Sullivan finally selected her real-life hero, she wouldn't choose me. And, as a result, she wouldn't be living the happily-ever-after that had been planned for us since we were kids.

I felt bad for her.

But then again, Megan had stomped on my heart and flattened my pretty healthy ego on New Year's Day. I figured I was finally walking the road to recovery.

It's time to purge Megan Sullivan from my heart and soul forever.

I only hoped I was up to the acting job.

# 3

*Megan*

FRIDAY AFTERNOON I HAD my aura read by a psychic.

Like many of you, I generally shied away from any activity that might remotely resemble having my head shrunk. But since my close encounter with Jack Spencer on Tuesday, I couldn't get him out of my mind. I'd gone from dreaming about him almost nightly to thinking about him practically constantly.

Maybe the psychic could help.

Her name was Vanessa and she came highly recommended. In addition to her quarter-page ad in the Yellow Pages, Vanessa recently had been featured on Cable Z, and she wrote a weekly column for one of the alternative tabloids. She also took cash, checks and all major credit cards.

I told no one where I was going. I didn't want to hear a chorus of snickers.

The reading went like this: I just dropped by around three. According to the phone book ad, no appointment was necessary because, being a psychic, Vanessa knew I was coming and had set aside thirty minutes for my reading.

Her ash-blond hair was pulled back from her face, revealing model-like cheekbones in an ageless, wrinkle-free complexion. She wore a flowing gown that reminded me of a kimono, but was wispy, sheer and flowed around her in a way that made me think a slight breeze was hard at work keeping her safe from bad vibes.

Vanessa read auras, palms and her crystal ball in a tiny Chelsea storefront just a few doors down from Spencer's. She invited me to sit at a small, round table covered by a beautiful white lace cloth, poured some green tea into huge clay mugs, lit a few jasmine candles and suggested I get comfortable. I was already imagining how comfortable I'd be getting with a piece of Spencer's cheesecake in less than an hour.

The highlights:

"You're stressed," she said.

My clenched fists on the table were a dead giveaway.

She pressed a nerve on the top of each hand, and I relaxed. She took both of my hands in hers.

"Ah, an Aries," she offered with a Yoda-like smile. "Youthful outlook, enthusiastic participant, a woman who loves to argue and seeks great adventures."

So far, five for five. I was impressed.

Vanessa: You're an artist, with a great vision you long to share with the world.

Me: Interior design. I've just started my own business.

Vanessa: And you're working too hard. A classic Aries trait. Overachieving can cause stress.

Me: You sound like Chloe. And Patty.

Vanessa: What they say has meaning to you. But something is missing. Love, perhaps? Is there a new man in your life? Or maybe not?

Me (adamantly): I'm not in love. There is no man.

(I'd jump back into the dating pool. When I was ready. Not that I still mourned the what-might-have-beens with Trey. But I was going to be cautious before falling in love/lust again.)

Vanessa: Ah, stubborn. If he says yes, you say no. Doesn't matter how you really feel, because it's not just the thrill of the argument, it's the thrill of the argument with him.

Me (forcefully): There is no man. I'm not in love.

Vanessa (her finger tracing my love line): It's broken. And you're in pain.

Me: Can you loosen your grip a little?

Vanessa (peering closely at my love line): I see a tiny fork in the road to romance forming. Your heart has been cracked, not broken. You have strong feelings that will burn to the surface.

Me: He makes me crazy. (Pause) I slept with him.

Vanessa: Him?

Me (giving a little detail): Jack. You know.

Vanessa (nodding and closing her eyes): Still, you are impulsive. Very impulsive. And that is why you ultimately said yes. And will say yes again and again. Even when you say no, you mean yes.

Me: I don't want to say yes. And when I say no, it's no.

There I was, arguing. For the sake of an argument.

Vanessa: You've no choice. Neither does he. Because Jack Spencer is your destiny or your downfall.

Okay, I know what you're thinking. That I needed a psychic to tell me what I already knew? That if I let a little bit of Jack Spencer back into my life, that little bit would mutate and speed-grow like a virus until he was all over the place?

Then it hit me.

Could Vanessa be a *real* psychic? She'd never met me before today. So how the heck did she know the Jack I was talking about was Jack Spencer?

In a bit of a daze, I thanked her, paid her fee (fifty bucks) and left a generous tip. On the way home, I found myself passing by Spencer's and walking the few blocks to the nearest grocery, where I bought two pints of mint chocolate chip ice cream. When I got to my apartment, I turned on the AC as high as it would go, put on my flannel nightshirt and wrapped myself in my down comforter and around my Maine coon cat. Then I indulged in every bittersweet morsel of ice cream until I hit the bottom of the first carton.

Before starting on pint two, I called my big sis, Patty.

"I need to talk." I tried to keep desperation out of my voice and still be heard above kids screaming in the background.

"Now is not a good time," she said. "Can it wait until the weekend?" Then a muffled scream. "Lisa! You are not going out of this house dressed like that!"

"I'll need a full hour on Sunday," I warned.

"Just bring cheesecake," said Patty, the only member of my family in whom I'd confided some of the details about you know what with you know who, "and we can pig out and dish about you know who until dawn."

I hated to say I counted the hours until Sunday. But I did.

Sundays have always been sacred Sullivan family days, and unless a member of my boisterous family woke up not breathing, his/her presence was expected at my parents' dinner table.

If you're ever invited, don't try showing up at five, eating at six and leaving at seven. We're talking showing up at three at the latest (preferably two) and leaving when my mother said it's time. Which could very well be the next morning. (Hello, bitch of a commute back to the city!)

This particular afternoon, the train pulled into the Montclair station on time (precisely one twenty-seven), and I was the only passenger to get off. It's the same train I'd ridden every Sunday since I graduated from college, because as you could plainly see, I was still breathing.

Even on Sundays the station parking lot was packed tight, like sardines, with cars, vans and SUVs. You'd think that after forty-hour-plus crazed work weeks in Manhattan (add in nearly three hours daily of commute time), suburbanites would have saner things to do than trek back into the city voluntarily. Especially with the kids.

On the other hand, why would any card-carrying city dweller voluntarily come out to the 'burbs on a beautiful, late spring weekend, rather than bask in the sun on the green grass of Central Park, or rollerblade along the banks of the Hudson River? Or clean the kitchen, scrub down the bathroom and replace the cat box litter?

We do it because we love our mothers.

The trip was also a one-stop family visit, as my sisters, Patty and Ellyn, lived in Montclair with their families. Within hollering distance of my parents' home. It works for them so that's all that matters.

According to the *New York Times*, Montclair was "Jersey chic." It had parks, trees, superb schools, a quaint shopping area, a good family-style pizza parlor, where extra cheese didn't cost extra, and was in driving distance of any and all the chain stores or malls—if that's your shopping thing.

My parents' Tudor-style home, located in a gated community and on a cul-de-sac, was within walking distance of the station. It didn't take me long to navigate through the parking lot and over the two blocks to Montclair Estates.

I tapped lightly on the window at the guard station, which seemed to jog the man out of his stupor. He nodded and waved me through while he remained im-

mersed in golf on his palm-sized TV. I could have been
a knife-wielding, homicidal maniac and he'd have ab-
sently passed me through unless I'd arrived at a commercial break.

Ah, yes, the suburbs!

As usual, my fan club awaited me.

Gathered were my four nieces: Patty's girls (Lisa the
budding fashionista, nine, and the three-year-old twins,
Emilie and Rose); and Ellyn's five-year-old Diana. Plus
my two nephews: Ellyn's twin toddlers, Alec and Matt,
who were just starting to toddle at age one, but who were
smartly buckled into their double stroller, chocolate
smeared all over their cherubic faces.

After the shouted hellos, the warm hugs and inevitable
sticky kisses, the kids seemed to forget I was there. I loved
these little people, but a small dose of them went a long
way. Which was another way of saying I wasn't ready for
motherhood.

Behind them stood Patty—another redhead and five
years my elder—who'd never learned to boil water but
was dynamite in dealing with quarks. In addition to full-
time mothering and sister counseling, she taught physics
part-time at Princeton.

I could read Patty's face easier and faster than I could
read any book, and from the conflicting worried and anxious looks she tossed my way, I knew something big-
time was wrong. And that our sisterly chat would have
to wait.

"Tell me!"

"Start back to Grandma's," she called out to the children
with a bit of forced liveliness, and yanked me off to the side.

The parade moved forward. Patty and I lagged a bit
behind.

"Promise me you won't get on the next train back to the city." She grabbed my arm in a viselike hold.

Uh-oh. It's worse than wrong. It's bad.

"I promise."

"The Spencers are here."

"The Spencers are here a lot."

"Jack brought them."

"He usually does." And recently has had the smarts to disappear before I arrived.

"Jack's still at the house."

I came to an abrupt stop. "I'll wait here until he leaves."

I wanted to talk about him. About my confused feelings for him. About how I was tricked into working with him. Not see him. Obviously, the Spencers had gotten a late start from the city, and it was taking Jack a little longer to bust out of there.

He was, as my mother fondly put it—and no offense to my brothers-in-law—the son she never had. And if she had to choose between the two of us, I'm not sure she'd be able to do it.

"He's staying, not leaving."

"I'm leaving, not staying."

"You promised."

She had me there. Promises were not something my family took lightly. (I'd promised my mother and Jack's that I'd take a look at the Spencer apartment, and look where that landed me—visiting a psychic.) "I can't see him. I had my one Jack Spencer sighting for the week. That was Tuesday. When he was supposed to be working."

"Gotcha!" Patty pointed out with a smile. "Today's Sunday, the beginning of another week."

"I hate you."

"I hate you back."

We sighed and continued walking.

"Sunday dinner's turned into a goodbye party for the Spencers," Patty said. "When the two Ritas asked him to stay—"

"Asked him?" I've never known the two Ritas to *ask* anything. Plead. Cajole. Threaten. All done within the bounds of motherly love. The two of them don't know the meaning of leaving well enough alone.

Patty shrugged. "Let's just say they made him an offer he couldn't refuse. His parents are moving to Florida tomorrow, after all, so you can't blame this one on Jack."

Wanna bet? "I'll need you to be my buffer."

"It'll cost you."

Of course. "What this time?"

"New wallpaper in the kids' bathroom."

"How soon?"

"Next weekend? I ordered the stuff online and it arrived yesterday. If you take an earlier train, you could probably have the paper up by dinner."

"Deal." Patty was prime buffer material because, as daughter number one, she's had the most experience. And, since Montclair was permanently stamped in my date book for Sundays, it's not like I had any big plans in mind.

All too soon, we were at the house. Usually I marveled at the perfection of the English-style garden, but not today.

Parked in front of the perfectly groomed lawn was a late-model Ford with New York plates, a tank of a car that was definitely not Jack's taste or style. But it was the only kind of car his parents felt safe riding in (aka, a car that a breeze wouldn't blow off the George Washington Bridge and into the Hudson).

Jack lazed on the hood of the car, leaning back on his elbows, eyes covered by reflective sunglasses, obviously lost in some world of his own.

If you repeat the following and/or attribute any of it to me, you're history.

For a moment, I wanted to be up on that car hood with Jack, his arm draped around my shoulders, his lips nuzzling the sensitive spot on my neck, just below my ear.

Could Vanessa be right? That when I said no, I meant yes?

I really needed to think seriously about having sex very soon, with a man who wasn't Jack Spencer.

He slid off the hood of the car. Dressed in faded tight jeans and a white T-shirt that hugged his muscles (obviously he'd been working out; how did I miss that on Tuesday?), he looked like one of the romance novel heroes I'd become involved with (tall, dark, dangerous) until I found a man who didn't find his wedding planner more intriguing than his fiancée.

"Jack."

"Megan."

He didn't remove his sunglasses, but I could feel the heat of his gaze as it locked on mine. Followed by a sizzle of electricity, one that I couldn't blame on the Jersey power company. The lines in this development were buried underground.

I glanced over at Patty, who watched both of us with a curious expression on her face.

"You know, Megan," she said with a crafty smile, "I don't think the kids' bathroom needs new wallpaper after all."

Traitor. I always knew she had a soft spot in her heart for Jack, and would turn on me on a dime. I'd foolishly expected she'd listen to my side of the story first. Then Jack's. And then she'd tell *me* I was right.

Since family never walked into the house through the front door, we (me, Patty, the kids and Jack) made our way around to the huge, sprawling backyard that was fenced in for privacy.

I'd barely gotten the gate latch open when I was greeted by loud barks. Leading the pack was Webster, my parents' three-year-old golden retriever, followed by Oscar, the Jack Russell terrier puppy that owned my sister Ellyn's family.

And then there was Achilles, who'd obviously come along to New Jersey for a ride and had made some new canine friends. The Great Dane raced over and prepared to bowl us over.

"Heel." Jack ordered.

The puppy jumped up and slobbered all over my face.

"Heel." Jack pointed to his side. Achilles finished his wet kiss, then rolled onto his back.

"He's still in training," Jack muttered as he leaned over and scratched the puppy's belly and ears.

Aren't we all?

I picked up the chewed-up tennis ball that the relatively more sedate Oscar dropped at my feet, and tossed it toward the back of the yard. All three dogs were off and running, and I joined the kids and Jack's dad, who was setting up the grill.

"So, Jack," my dad called out from his favorite spot in the yard, the hammock that hung between two massive oak trees, "let me take a look at those papers you mentioned."

Jack headed over to join my dad. Patrick Sullivan was still brawny and active at sixty-five. He had recently retired as chief legal counsel of a Fortune 500 company after more than thirty years, but still did some work for private clients and family.

Curiosity had me following.

"You're his lawyer?" I asked Dad, as Jack pulled some papers out of his back pocket and handed them over. I recognized the letterhead—Design Time. Uh-oh. "What gives?"

"Client confidentiality." My dad nudged me off the spot I'd claimed on the hammock.

"It's not like I don't know what the proposal and contract say," I told them both. "I wrote them."

"And now I'm going to look them over," he said mildly. "Go annoy your mother so I can have a few words with Jack."

"I can't believe this," I hissed at Jack. "Why not take an ad out in the *New York Times* announcing you don't trust me."

"It's nothing personal," Jack said. "Just good business."

Don't you just hate platitudes? "It might be just good business to you, but this business is pretty personal to me." Anyway, I couldn't explain that I didn't want my father to know how much I was going to charge Jack for my time and expertise.

He would lecture me for undervaluing both.

"Let me refresh your memory." Jack tapped the side of my forehead. "'P.S. I'm going to take you to the financial cleaners.'"

There was that.

Since neither of the Ritas was in plain sight, I wandered over in the direction of Patty and her husband Jake, who were chilling out on the flagstone patio. (Ellyn and Tom had been blessed with a motherly dispensation to arrive late because they were attending an afternoon wedding.) I'm fond of both brothers-in-law. They're nice guys and very adept at insect disposal, a trait I much admire in a man.

"Hear you and Jack are thinking about finally making whatever it is between you two legal." Jake practiced being a comedian on the side.

"You are so not funny," I deadpanned.

Patty slapped her husband on the top of his head. "Ignore him. He's just jealous because he'd love to get his hands on the furniture in that apartment. For some reason, Jake has bonded with the seventies." Patty shuddered.

Jake collected antiques, refinished them and then sold them at a healthy profit. He owned a classy shop here in Montclair, one that I'd relied on many times when searching for just the right piece for the right client and the right home.

In return, Jake had referred some business to Design Time.

Isn't networking grand?

I went off to find the two Ritas, who were busy slicing up veggies in the kitchen. Rita 1, my mother, is petite with red hair and at sixty hasn't lost a bit of her grit.

Rita 2, Jack's mom, recently celebrated her sixty-second birthday. She's tiny, doll-like, and had gone gray naturally since she was diagnosed with breast cancer last year and lost most of her long, thick, chestnut-brown hair to aggressive chemotherapy. She seemed tired, and a bit pale, and I knew she was looking forward to a calmer, simpler lifestyle in Florida.

"So, Megan, I've got some good news," said Rita 2. "My Jack is going to be on that biography TV show, you know, the one where they say, 'Every life has a story.' "

"Today?" I twirled in panic. Sucked in a deep breath when I realized there were no TV cameras or sneaky reporters in sight. Not that I didn't think my family would have neglected to warn me, but, then again…

"A few months from now," said Rita 2. "But me and your mother, we gotta prepare. So?"

"Hmm" seemed the safest response. Rita 2 was proud of Jack, and I couldn't fault her for that. But I'm neither a celebrity watcher nor a celebrity hanger-on—those kinds of TV shows turned me off, because I truly believed in the "private" part of private lives.

I grabbed a can of diet soda from the refrigerator and found the shelves stacked with ground sirloin patties, deboned chicken breasts and all-beef hotdogs.

It seemed we were having a picnic.

Rita 1 handed me a knife and pointed to the pot of boiled potatoes. Rita 2 took the knife from my hand, pushed me into a chair at the kitchen table and started slicing potatoes. (The potato salad at Spencer's is Rita 2's secret recipe, one she refused to share despite my promises to name my firstborn after her, and I've never tasted better. I fear the only way to get the recipe is to marry into the family.)

"So, Megan," Rita 2 pressed again, "you'll go on this TV show and say nice things about Jack."

I plucked a piece of celery from the platter on the table. "They can't find someone who actually has nice things to say?"

Rita 1 shook her head. "You don't mean that."

Rita 2 laid the knife on the table and took my hand in both of hers. "How could the mother of my future grandchildren say that about the father of my future grandchildren?"

Have I mentioned that both Ritas are in denial?

I glanced up at my mother, whose look of mild reproach had me mentally squirming. She was more protective of Rita 2 than of her natural born children.

"Sure," I said. After all, what's another capitulation if it made the Ritas happy? And if the fates were smiling, my phone would be out of order if/when somebody called. "If whoever's putting Jack's biography together wants a testimonial, I'll testify on his behalf."

It was what they wanted to hear, and reminded me once again of Vanessa's words: *You say no but mean yes.*

Sigh.

Dinner was, as usual, a mixture of good company, fine food and spirited conversation.

The Ritas knew better than to mention anything that would remind me of my aborted wedding. Or still-single state.

But they hammered away at Jack.

He was quiet, although both Ritas tried valiantly to stir him up. They succeeded, finally, when they started questioning him about his love life as portrayed in the gossip rags (and with some Hollywood PR-type named Sheli). He dropped his sunglasses from his forehead, to cover his eyes, and crossed his arms at his chest.

Even the children could see the Ritas had gone too far. The kids disappeared fast into the far reaches of the backyard.

The Ritas subsided. That is, until after dinner.

The sun had nearly set when both Ritas suggested coyly that Jack and I take a walk.

"It's a full moon tonight."

"You young people should have some time to yourselves."

"Whatever problems you're having, talk."

"You must have something to talk about."

"Do it for us."

Jack jerked up out of his lawn chair, grabbed my hand and yanked me out of mine. "Let's take a walk," he said with a lack of graciousness that told me how angry he was. But I couldn't blame him. I couldn't take any more of this motherly meddling either.

He started walking.

My feet followed his.

Achilles trailed after us both, and I just managed to latch onto the dog leash before Jack strode through the back gate.

He crossed my parents' lawn and headed toward the far side of the cul-de-sac. Once we were on the lighted flagstone path that led to the community's play area, he dropped my hand. And I secured the leash around Achilles' collar.

The playground was fully lit, as well.

Jack plopped down on one side of the child-size teetertotter and wordlessly pointed to the other. I climbed aboard. It seemed childish not to.

I waited. And Achilles waited. And finally heeled, without command, at Jack's side. And when a good, long silence had elapsed, Jack pushed up on his end of the teeter-totter, nearly tossing me off mine. I could tell he was fighting his mad, and that the mad was winning.

"Sorry," he said, not sounding a bit sorry. "Been a while since I've tamed one of these beasts."

I wasn't in the mood for a teeter-totter war, but since Jack outweighed me by more than seventy pounds, the advantage was pretty much his. My next move wasn't planned, at least not intentionally. I pushed up, hard and fast. And Jack, who'd let go of the metal balance handle, careened forward so quickly, he practically somersaulted into my lap.

He straddled the wooden teeter-totter less than a foot in front of me, breathing heavily. "What is it," he asked between gulping in air, "that makes otherwise intelligent adults devolve back into children when they're in a playground?"

"Our parents' expectations."

"Yeah." He didn't seem happy with my explanation.

"I'm sorry."

"Care to elaborate?"

"I'm sorry you didn't fall flat on your ass."

That brought out a reluctant smile. "Ah, Megan, you always knew how to make me laugh, even when you were mocking me."

Was I justified in acting the shrew? Guess it depends on your point of view. If I was going to work for Jack—and that hefty fifteen percent commission—then he deserved the best of me, not the worst.

"I like your design thoughts."

He offered another smile, this one with dimples. "Not the Tarzan-Jane decor you were expecting."

I cocked a brow.

"You know—leopard carpeting, black vinyl bedspread, gold-flocked wallpaper, mirror over a king-size water bed."

"I figured if you could dress yourself fashionably, you could dress a room competently."

"A compliment."

"A fact. Your taste has never been in question here."

"Just my behavior."

Oops! Talk about going for the grand slam.

"If we're going to work together, *if*," I stressed, "then our private lives are off-limits. This is strictly business."

"I haven't officially offered you the job."

He had a point there. I shrugged. "Let me know what you decide. We'll see if Design Time can fit you into our crowded schedule. I'm sure Dad will tell you the contract is fair."

"I want this to work."

Yes, no. No, yes.

"We're both professionals." I started back toward my parents' house.

"Megan."

I stopped dead in my tracks. Took a calming breath, then another. I wasn't about to go anywhere else with Jack tonight, especially into personal matters. "It's getting late, Jack. The Ritas will be wondering where we are."

"The Ritas know exactly where we are."

And the Ritas knew exactly what they were doing when a few moments later they suggested that it would be safer, and quicker, for Jack to drive me back to the city.

Both of us were exhausted.

Neither of us had the energy to refuse.

Jack, in his good son portrayal—which would have been perfect for a cable Movie of the Week—thanked my mother for the great dinner. He hugged his parents, wished them a safe trip to Florida in the morning and promised to keep his cell phone on so they could call him when they arrived.

Me, never the actress, could have taken home an Oscar for Best Mental Restraint when I kept from strangling my mother as she kissed me, told me that she had my best interests at heart and then slammed the car door shut with these parting words:

"Have a nice night, you two."

As though we were heading off to a happily ever after.

The ride back to the city was uneventful. Achilles jumped from the back seat to snuggle between the two of us. Smart dog.

Jack was silent.

Me, too.

Well, I guess we'd already talked ourselves out, and far as I could tell, no useful information had been exchanged. A far cry from the days when we used to tell each other everything.

He pulled up to the front of my building less than an hour

later, and let the car idle in Park. He got out and sprinted around the back of the Ford and opened my car door.

I stepped onto the curb. "Who's Sheli?"

"A girl."

"I certainly hope so."

"A woman I've been seeing." Pause. "Seriously."

Talk about a punch to the gut, and then some. I'd have to think about my reaction later. Right now, I had some questions.

"She local? Do I know her?"

"I met her in L.A. She's moving to the city next month."

"Do I need to talk with her before choosing countertops and paint colors?"

A slight hesitation, then, "That might not be a bad idea."

My heart dropped to my stomach in a free fall worthy of a Disney World thrill ride. "I'd enjoy meeting her. I'm sure she's everything you deserve."

Jack said nothing. The fact that in the glare of the street-lights, I could see the look on his face run the spectrum from amusement to indifference and something I couldn't quite identify, bothered me a lot.

I turned to head into my building, and felt Jack's hand press lightly on my shoulder. He came up behind me and kissed my neck. And then my cheek. And then my lips. Not just once, but twice. Then I lost count.

And I let him kiss me. No, that's not accurate. I fully participated, tongue on tongue, grope matching grope, until we were both breathless. And our clothes were a bit mussed.

Jack didn't say a word. But I could tell that he wasn't happy with himself. Or me.

"That's not going to happen again," he insisted, as he got back into the car. "I mean it." He sped off down the street.

I sat on the steps until long after the taillights had faded into the distance.

What, I wondered, would Vanessa the psychic have to say about this?

# 4

*Jack*

THERE WAS NO REASONABLE explanation for why I kissed Megan. Other than, some alien creature took over my mind and body for a few minutes the other night, and did what I was thinking I'd like to do but had promised myself I wasn't going to do.

I had no idea what Megan was thinking or feeling about our kiss(es)—or about anything else—these days. Our three conversations since The Kiss haven't been in real time. Because over the past seventy-two or so hours, we've been communicating the modern way.

E-mail. V-mail. Express mail.

We're getting together tonight at six, at a neighborhood tapas bar called Cleo's, just a stone's throw from the Seventy-second Street subway station where Amsterdam meets Broadway.

Her request to meet was made, and I answered (by e-mail). The location determined (after several v-mails). Now that the contract has been vetted and signed (thanks to express mail), we're moving at lightning speed here.

The plan was to review Megan's preliminary design concepts for the apartment, which, I should note, was located nearly twenty blocks north of our meeting place. Wouldn't you agree that it would have made more sense to meet up at the apartment? Maybe walk through the space, so I could pretend to understand what it was going to look like?

But, rather than argue, I'd gone along with Megan's suggestion. I just hoped I wasn't hit by another tidal wave of the weird (and conflicting) emotions I'd been battling since my relationship with Megan crashed big-time. Or that another alien being would possess me.

Megan and I were certainly living on different planets. Except when it came to foreplay and sex: I hadn't been the only one panting heavily when she (finally) eased out of my arms and dashed up the steps to her front door.

Meanwhile, back to my reality, or what passed for reality in the world of TV crime-drama. It was shortly before dawn and I (sipping my third cup of coffee) was watching as my stunt double earned his combat pay, performing a fistfight on the deck of a yacht on its way to a rendezvous with destiny. Or a dead body.

Which, considering the state of network TV, was likely both. I didn't write the scripts; I just learned the lines as they tossed 'em my way.

Location shooting was fun. Not only was it a change of pace (from the sterile courthouse set down in Chelsea), it forced me to visit areas of the city I'd never think to check out on my own. This morning we were filming up at The Cloisters, one of the city's unique landmarks, a former monastery turned art museum located near the northern tip of Manhattan, in a forest of trees that most city dwellers never see up close and personal.

No makeup needed. I was wearing my own clothes: jeans, a T-shirt and ratty tennis shoes. The scene called for me to be rumpled, stubbled and gritty-eyed. Not much acting required, because after the courier woke me around midnight to deliver the new script pages and I'd learned my meager number of lines, I'd been unable to fall back asleep. Today's work would translate into less than three minutes of airtime, most of them action, with very little dialogue. Given my lack of sleep, that was just as well.

According to pages forty-one through forty-six of the shooting script, we opened after the commercial with an establishing shot of the yacht slowly making its way up the Hudson to the boathouse. The lights of Manhattan highlighted two men on the yacht who were punching each other senseless as the boat headed toward shore.

Cut to a close-up of A.D.A. Logan Hunter, cheeks unshaven, hair mussed, a bit of blood on his face. He leaped to the dock, barely making it. A gunshot pierced the silence. Cut to the other man, lying motionless on the boat. Cut to a path leading to The Cloisters.

Logan approached carefully, and saw the beautiful Detective Caitlin O'Connor, gun in hand. Some nonsensical dialogue. The two—faithful viewers knew—have been inseparable the past few episodes, but haven't done It. Some penetrating, longing looks. Caitlin handed Logan the extra gun she just happened to have stashed in the lacy garter on her thigh. The two separated. Logan turned left, Caitlin right.

The camera lingered a nanosecond on the spot where the two almost-lovers stood. There was another shot. Bang!

And we turned the page to find…nothing but blank pages from forty-seven until fifty-two (ostensibly the end) where the dialogue and other stuff normally went.

Uh-oh.

Did I mention this episode was the first of a two-part season finale, generally known as a cliff-hanger?

Did I mention the network honchos came to visit last week?

Did I mention that, although *The D.A. Chronicles* consistently ranks in Nielsen's top ten, those honchos wanted to make some "artistic" changes?

Did I mention that, despite my guaranteed four-year contract, I'm slightly paranoid about job security?

While the scene on the yacht was shot from several vantage points (my close-ups will come later), I was seated in a director's-style chair surrounded by Caitlin (her real name's her character's name—long story, don't ask) and Sam. Hanging around were several extras, the costume czarina Rachel and my makeup fairy godmother Alicia, who was busy painting her fingernails ten different neon colors.

We were slurping the extra-strong coffee, watching as the techies tried to fix whatever was wrong with the lights. We'd been waiting more than an hour to film the part of the scene I'll refer to as "almost-lovers parting before commercial break."

The mood here flowed from agitated to edgy. No one spoke. There were more than forty people on set, and if you hadn't seen the blank script pages by now, you'd heard about 'em. Our director and his minions were MIA. Not a good sign.

Cut to an hour or so later. The sun had risen midway in the sky, the caffeine was shooting through my bloodstream faster than the express train down Broadway and we were still waiting.

Sam broke the silence with a heavy sigh. "One of us is history."

Caitlin fussed in her chair. "They won't get rid of me."

"And why is that?" sniped Rachel, who had been heard

to loudly complain that for a model, the blond, dewy-eyed Caitlin had no fashion sense. Or sense of any kind.

"I'm the only woman in this cast of Neanderthals," Caitlin sniffed.

I wasn't gonna be the one to explain the facts of acting life. They could kill off her character outright—aka getting rid of one woman and replacing her with another to keep the balance. Or they could put her character on life support, and when she woke up, she neither remembered what happened (nor even looked the same).

On the other hand, there's last hired, first fired (me).

Maybe it was time to v-mail my high-powered agent, and see where he was re: negotiating that cable TV movie to fill up my hiatus time. I dug my cell phone from my pocket, powered up and saw I had a text message.

*Call me. Urgent. M.*

I punched out her number.

"Jack." She sounded perky and rushed. "Hope I'm not interrupting filming."

"We're on a break." Understatement. "What's urgent?" (Was trying to keep Tough Guy-cool here.)

Slight pause. "I have to cancel you. I have a meeting with a client."

I was about to say, "I'm a client, too," but I held back. So, she's just gonna erase me off her calendar? Too bad I didn't think of it first. I tried for nonchalant. *Acting.* "Let's meet later tonight."

"Um, well, that won't work. I was hoping we could do a quick lunch."

"I'm on location today. Up at The Cloisters." I glanced around the set. The way the production staff kept huddling, it didn't look like filming would begin anytime soon. We probably had time for several lunches.

The big clock on The Cloisters tower struck ten. "Can you get up here by noon?"

"Sure." No hesitation.

So maybe she really did have to cancel, and it wasn't just an excuse to avoid seeing me. Maybe she really wanted to see me that bad. Good sign? Bad sign? These days, who knew.

"I'll ask one of the production assistants to meet you at the subway station and bring you on over to the set," I told her. "Just look for someone dressed like an underpaid gofer."

A pause. "I'll take a cab."

"You could," I said reasonably, "but the subway's faster and cheaper."

"I'd be more comfortable in a cab."

"Megan, do whatever pleases you. I'll pay for the cab."

"I can afford it."

"I'm not saying you can't. Just add it to my bill. As a business expense."

Pause. "I'll take the subway."

I challenge you to find the logic there. But that was Megan, arguing for the sake of arguing. It used to amuse me. Now it annoyed me. Yet another sign our relationship had taken a wrong turn.

"Jack?"

"I'm still here." I waited for what was next.

"I just know you're going to love the design."

Before I could forget my role and get all mushy in return, Megan clicked off.

As luck would have it, within the next hour all technical problems seemed to fix themselves, and we were ready to roll. Except the script called for the scene to be shot shortly before dawn. It was now nearing noon.

What to do? There's a longtime movie trick, called "day-for-night," where special filters on the camera lens make the film think it's four in the morning, rather than daytime. We rehearsed the scene (see above) until our director was convinced of its artistic integrity. He called, "Cut." We broke for lunch.

And I turned to see Megan Sullivan hovering off set.

Here's what struck me:

Megan wasn't dressed for business (her man-killer cream suit and peach camisole).

She wasn't dressed for play (her walking shorts that showed off her long legs and sleeveless T that molded her nicely rounded breasts).

Instead she was dressed in a sleeveless cotton sundress made for, dare I even think it, seduction?

Remember Sheli? I was trying, and it wasn't easy.

Among the many reasons I was a fan of the coming of summer was the prospect of seeing women in sundresses. Megan's was a blue and white cotton number, with a scooped-out neckline and buttons racing down from a spot that teased her cleavage to stop just below her knees. Slender ankles. Bare feet. And sandals. One of those secret aphrodisiacs, especially when women painted their toenails.

Megan's curly red hair was pulled into a ponytail, but wisps had managed to escape and frame her face. I couldn't see her green eyes, which were hidden by sunglasses. As were her freckles.

The breeze played with the skirt of her dress, revealing a hint of nicely toned leg. But not that other bunch of freckles located very high on her right thigh. (I was trying hard not to think that at least one other man knew their location.)

My heart thumped against my chest. My groin tightened in that way that makes wearing snug jeans just a *little* dicey.

I caught her gaze, waved her over.

Before I could offer Megan my canvas chair (with my name stenciled on the back), Sam dragged one over. With the words Guest Star stenciled on the back.

"This is so neat." She smiled warmly at Sam and nestled into the chair. "I've never been—what do you call it?—on location before."

I handled the introductions. "Sam. Caitlin. Alicia. Rachel."

A chorus of "Hi, Hello," and then silence. Which surprised me, because this group was *never* quiet.

"Did I come at a bad time?" Megan addressed the question to no one in particular.

"No, no, no," Sam said, a bit too heartily. "It's good to meet you. Finally. You're all Jack's yakking about these days."

Thanks, buddy.

"He means, I'm boring everyone with the renovation plans," I said.

"We're never going to get outta here by five." Caitlin pursed her collagen-treated lips. "And I have a cover shoot for *Chic*. No way am I not going to be there."

"It'll all work out." I tried to play peacemaker, knowing if Caitlin got going I'd never get a chance to discuss my renovation with Megan.

"What time is it?" Rachel shook her wrist and stared at her watch. "I'm supposed to dress Caitlin for that *Chic* cover shoot. And I won't be rushed."

"Let's eat now, worry later," I suggested, and led the parade to the deli buffet (catered daily by Spencer's long before I joined the cast) that had been set up in a parklike area near the entrance to The Cloisters.

One of the PR types from the network hung around

nervously, expecting, I suppose, that we acting heathens would suddenly take off through the museum with our food, spraying mayo, mustard or whatever on the walls. To which an art critic with a discerning eye would declare a masterpiece in this Friday's *Times*. Or not.

I expertly assembled a pastrami and Swiss on rye (with dark mustard) for myself, and observed Megan as she squeezed a dollop of mayo onto her smoked turkey (lettuce, no cheese) on whole wheat. Grabbing a pint container of potato salad, napkins, forks and two diet sodas, I found a quiet spot under one of the big oak trees that dotted the property.

And so we were alone.

Megan sat cross-legged next to me, her back against the tree, the skirt of her dress draping her knees. "I like your friends."

"That's good," I noted dryly, as Sam, Rachel and Alicia spotted us. I shot Sam a look that said, "No way," and he shrugged helplessly as Rachel and Alicia hurried over. He followed. "Because they're coming to lunch with us."

It seemed we weren't going to be graced with Caitlin's presence, but then I guess she decided the alternative to eating with all of us was eating alone. And so she joined the group. And strategically placed herself directly across from me. It was going to be a long, *long* lunch.

Megan shrugged. "Won't hurt to get their thoughts. They might see something you don't."

Translation: Despite what I said earlier, that you have some fashion sense, you really have no taste, no style, and now we're gonna prove it. In front of people you call friends.

Megan set her sandwich aside, dug into her straw tote and retrieved a pad and pen. She looked up to find four pairs of eyes staring at her expectantly. She glanced my way. I shrugged.

"Would one of you like to take notes?" Megan asked a bit hesitantly.

Alicia's hand shot into the air first. When Megan handed her the pad and pen, Caitlin shot me a murderous glare (as usual, she was auditioning for a role and wasn't happy about the rejection). Sam rolled his eyes. And Rachel wandered off.

Megan opened her portfolio so the two sides lay flat, and carefully spread huge sheets of manila drawing paper—filled with colors and squiggles—so everyone could take a good look.

Like many city dwellers I know, the closest I've come to major power tools was catching HGTV at my parents' place, and observing the pros on *This Old House* or *Fix It Up!* I watched the shows with my dad. We called it our father-son bonding hour.

While I can do Shakespeare, Miller or Mamet and get good notices, I'd flunk Reading Floor Plans 101.

We each played to our strengths.

Trust me, I had no idea what I was looking at. Or what I was supposed to say. So I was totally wingin' it here. My aim was to appear suave and knowledgeable, with a little nonchalance thrown in for good measure.

I picked up one sheet and examined it up close, then drew back to look at it from a distance. Little numbers I couldn't read. Little boxes bunched up against little boxes.

Megan plucked the paper from my hand and turned it horizontally. I peered over the top to see her trying to hide that she was a bit disappointed in my reaction. Or lack of one.

"Megan, these are terrific."

Sam! My man! Knew I could count on you!

Megan brightened. "You really think so?"

"You've opened up the space," Sam said. "Given it drama. A reason for being."

"Exactly. Look at this elevation."

Sam scooted next to her and examined the sheet. "Omigod! Turning that second kitchen into a library-study with built-ins is absolutely brilliant. I suppose you're thinking wide plank flooring instead of parquet here."

They both turned to me.

Sam cocked a brow in Megan's direction.

"Right!" I reluctantly set my sandwich down and enthused with as much enthusiasm as I could muster. I was an actor, so I acted.

She beamed.

I beamed right back, even though I had no idea what they'd been talking about, other than it sounded as though there would be a room somewhere in the apartment for my books, CDs and other guy toys.

Alicia, bless her, furiously took notes in a style of shorthand that looked just as Greek to me as the floor plans.

"You've seen the hovel he's living in?" Sam directed this question to Megan. "*House Beautiful* would never come calling there. But here. Definitely a visit, maybe even a cover story!"

Was I the only one who noticed that this question brought Caitlin out of whatever private world she'd been inhabiting since she'd joined us?

Or that maybe Sam was laying on the charm (and the compliments) a bit too thick?

Megan leaned toward Sam and whispered loudly. "Yes. It's so sad."

"It's not a hovel," I protested. I mean, a guy had to defend his crib vigorously, even if it was edging toward you know what. "It's a compact studio."

"A four-hundred-square-foot hovel," Sam pronounced. "With a patio. Its only saving grace."

"Almost five hundred," I muttered, determined to support my beleaguered apartment.

"Caitlin," Megan asked politely (and, in effect, changing the subject). "Any thoughts?"

"I think I'm done here." With a huff, she tossed the remains of her lunch in my lap. I guess Caitlin had read— and believed—a gossip column piece this morning dubbing us "an item," and considered Megan competition. What would she do when/if she heard about Sheli Bradshaw?

Not a wisp of truth, the Caitlin-and-me bit. I swear. Our characters might be on the brink of doing It, but Caitlin would never sleep between my real-life sheets.

On the other hand, if Megan thought that another woman thought I was a "get"…

Think about Sheli. A nice woman who not only likes you, but is moving to New York City for you. A woman who is not going to disappear after having sex.

"Ethan!" Sam yelled over to our set designer, who I assumed knew something about decorating since that's what he got paid for doing. More or less. "You gotta see the to-die-for floor plans for Jack's new apartment."

Would you believe that at the utterance of those two words, *floor plans*, several of my male co-workers stopped what they were doing and eagerly glanced our way?

Ethan Hancock drifted over, dressed in all black, from the sunglasses perched on his forehead to the tips of his high-tops (laces, too). He examined the floor plan in Sam's hand.

"I like the window placement," Ethan announced. "Good north and northwest exposure. Ceilings?"

"Twelve feet," Sam replied.

How the heck did he know?

"If we really wanted to make a statement," Sam said, "I'd say smash the plaster and make those babies floor-to-ceiling." He looked over to Megan for her reaction.

"Doable. But expensive."

"Write that down, Alicia," Sam ordered. "Floor-to-ceiling windows in the living room. Jack can afford it. Oooh, look at that."

He shuffled the floor plans so the before and after ones lay side by side. "All right! A few straight lines create a walk-in closet! Almost as huge as the kitchen, and with natural light."

I looked. It was. I faintly remembered telling Chloe I wanted a closet with a window (a joke). They'd figured out a way to make it happen. I was impressed.

By this time, we'd attracted the attention of the chief cinematographer, the assistant director, the assistant to the assistant director, the best boy, the gaffer and the gofer. Even Rachel had returned.

Alicia looked up from her notepad. "Color is an apartment's lifeblood," she announced dramatically. "Paint the kitchen—red!"

There was a moment of silence.

Then, as though cued, everyone spoke at once.

"Cherry!" Sam shouted over Ethan's, "A juicy apple!"

From the assistant director, "Raspberry! No, cranberry! No, raspberry."

"I love tomato!" Alicia held up a slice then bit into it.

The next offer was, "Peppers!" I think that suggestion

came from Sam, who, with a wink, told me he was definitely having a good time.

"Chilies!" said Rachel.

Red chilies? I couldn't keep up, but at least they were keeping with a food theme. And why did I feel as though I was at the Union Square Greenmarket, listening to the vendors as they tried to entice shoppers?

"How about radishes?" asked Alicia.

"Beets! Eggplant!" Ethan and the assistant director chimed in.

"Excuse me," Rachel said to Ethan. "I believe beets and eggplant are purple."

Ethan turned his sharp gaze on Rachel. "The same can be said of radishes. But they offer a contrasting color statement."

"You are so not fashionably cool," she responded.

I raised my hand, and my voice. "Enough debate over kitchen color. Red is…uh…red is right up there in my top…five…choices."

Everyone, it seemed, loved Megan's plans. And Alicia's initial color suggestion.

And I could see, from the flush of her cheeks and the smile on her face, that Megan was enjoying herself.

Everybody was having a good time. Was I the only guy in New York City unable to appreciate Megan's floor plans and thoughts of a red kitchen?

Nope. I wasn't.

A shadow crossed my shoulder, belonging to our director, Lionel Crosbie, a talented man with no discernable sense of humor but a truckload of Emmys, including two for our show. He dismissed the apartment plans with a wave of his hand. "If you're done playing house, Jack, we've a TV show to film before we go any more over budget." He paused. "Red? How yesterday."

Talk about popping a party balloon.

We cleaned up the remains of lunch. Note: I hadn't had a bite of my pastrami and Swiss on rye, nor a swallow of my mother's potato salad, so they were coming back to the set with me. An actor needed fuel to emote on cue.

Alicia handed the notebook back to Megan as though it was the Holy Grail, or an Emmy-winning script.

Everyone started to drift away, leaving Megan and me alone. "Wanna come watch?" I nodded in the direction of the set.

"I should get back to the office."

I smiled. "I'd like to see you."

"You're seeing me now."

"Tonight. After you meet with your client."

"Really, I can't. Other plans." She looked almost sorry. Or maybe the sunlight was playing tricks.

When she didn't elaborate, I pressed. "You've got a date?"

She straightened her shoulders, thinned her lips. "Yes."

"I didn't realize you had someone new in your life." You kissed me seventy-two hours ago like I was the only man left in the world.

"Jack, let it go."

I was trying, honestly. But somebody else was controlling the dialogue here. "Right."

"I'll see you Saturday."

Huh? First, you don't work weekends, and now you do? I hated it when the script kept changing and I couldn't keep up.

"At the apartment," she explained patiently. "The general contractor is coming at eleven. To examine your studs."

That sounded intriguing.

"Can't," I decided on the spur of the moment. "I'm working."

Actually, with the help of a few actor buddies, early Saturday morning I was finally moving my meager possessions, and Achilles, into 6-AB. And would definitely be there, up to my eyeballs in unpacked boxes. So I was stretching the definition of working. But Megan didn't have to know that.

If she was dating someone... How could I have missed the two Ritas' bulletin that Megan was dating? Just because her idiot fiancé hadn't appreciated her, didn't mean other idiots wouldn't be lining up for the chance to get Megan Sullivan naked and wet.

Or was this just Megan-style retaliation for my mentioning Sheli the other night?

I heard my name shouted by at least three people, and really had no choice but to get back to work. "I gotta go. Let me get someone to walk you back to the subway."

"I've got my cell. I'll just call a cab." She nudged me toward the set. "Go. They need you. I'll be fine."

I jogged back to the set, picked up my script. Checked and saw that pages forty-seven through fifty-two were still blank.

At the sound of a tooting horn, I looked up. A Yellow Cab was pulling out of the circular drive.

Was it my imagination, or did Megan look back at me longingly? But, then again, I was willing to believe in the concept of Santa Claus, the possibility of intelligent life on Mars and that some day I'd get my best friend back.

"You are so not worthy," Rachel hissed in a voice loud enough to wake the dead in neighboring New Jersey.

"All is not lost." Alicia patted her soothingly on the

# 5

*Megan*

GENERAL CONTRACTORS, like wedding planners, can be a girl's best friend, or her worst enemy.

Wedding planners can make or break a wedding.

General contractors can make or break a designer's career.

Get on the good side of your GC (do not alter major design decisions), and the project will finish on time and under budget. Get on his bad side (be indecisive), and expect to blow the budget and kiss client referrals goodbye. My worst experience was when the GC left the project weeks before completion because his wife found him with the client in an after-hours meeting (aka sex) surrounded by two-by-fours.

You know my feelings on wedding planners.

So when Neil Roberts, the busy CEO of Roberts Construction, barked over the phone that he could squeeze me in between eleven and noon on Saturday for a personal "look-see" at Jack's apartment, I agreed to the meeting.

I arrived at the apartment about twenty minutes early.

As I turned the key in the lock, I wondered what plans Jack had made for Achilles this morning. I'd made it clear in a v-mail that the dog was not invited to this party.

So, of course, the Great Dane welcomed me with loud barks, braced his paws on my shoulders and proceeded to tongue-wash my face.

"Don't be so impatient," a very familiar voice (belonging to a man who also wasn't supposed to be there) cheerfully called out. Jack stood under the archway leading to his bedroom, briskly rubbing his dark hair with one green towel and wearing nothing but a handkerchief-sized scrap of another, wrapped low around his waist.

I didn't need a camera to forever imprint that image of raw male sexuality in my mind. It was as though he'd just stepped out of a centerfold—or one of my nightly sexual fantasies.

Broad shoulders. Muscled chest. With a wiry mat of hair, shaped like an inverted triangle, that was beaded with water. And those long runner's legs. The last time I'd seen this much male skin, Jack had been buck naked and stretched out all over me, and around me.

Get a grip, Megan.

You're twenty-nine. You've seen naked male bodies before. You've slept with naked male bodies. You've slept with this body, belonging to this almost-naked male. There's nothing here you haven't seen, haven't explored.

And there is nothing good for you here. And you know it!

I shivered. But it wasn't from the air-conditioning, because the AC wasn't on. It was a shiver of pure lust.

I swallowed, hard. Then cleared my throat with a noise that sounded like I was choking.

Jack froze and peered out from under his towel. It was almost comical. Almost.

"You're early." He nonchalantly draped towel number one over his shoulder. And then checked to make sure towel number two was in its proper place.

"You're here."

"Observant *and* early. I thought I should hang around

to hear what the contractor says." A careless shrug of muscled shoulder. "All that brainstorming gave me some new ideas."

What a surprise. "Put some clothes on."

Jack cocked a brow that silently (and smugly) told me he knew he turned me on, then padded to his bedroom. I heard the door click shut.

Visual imagery is my business, so it wasn't hard to imagine Jack dropping the towel, stepping into boxers and… I couldn't continue because just thinking about what was going on in that bedroom turned my knees to mush.

Just so I wouldn't dare to take a peek, I decided to focus my visual attention on the apartment's living space. It was empty except for a floor lamp, minus its shade, and a love seat that looked like a prop from a low-budget horror movie. With Rita 2's lovely area rugs gone, the wood floor looked pitiful.

I could relate.

I waited long enough, I hoped, for Jack to get decent, then rapped lightly on the closed door. The slight pressure just about blew it open. Another item to add to my ever-expanding punch list of Things for Megan to Fix.

Jack stood at the curtainless window in profile, wearing jeans that rode tight and low on his lean hips. Yep, still sexy. And still off-limits.

"Where is everything?"

"Whatever couldn't fit in the bedroom here is in temporary storage. Except for a few things out there." He rummaged through a duffel and pulled on a T-shirt, then stuffed his feet into battered running shoes that he'd retrieved from under the unmade queen-size bed. "I'm living here. Got the plasma TV, the stereo. A corner for Achilles to hang out."

"You're living cramped." Along with the bed, he had a double dresser, a desk overrun by a computer and printer, an overstuffed chair that was losing the battle to keep its stuffing, plus two empty bookshelves. "Isn't this the chair that Rita 2 repeatedly threatened to beg Goodwill to take?"

He nodded. "Needs new insides and updated upholstery."

I thought Rita 2 was on target. The chair would have to go.

Jack gazed around the room. "More space here than in the studio. But I'm a little worried about Achilles. He's used to his patio. And it turns out he's not crazy about the elevator. And I'm not crazy about schlepping up and down five flights of stairs every time he wants to take a stroll to meet the poodle down the block."

Achilles, who'd parked himself on a pillow in his corner, looked up in interest at the mention of the poodle.

"Maybe you could train him to leap off the balcony and land on his feet. And then push on the doorbell so you can buzz him back inside after his date with Fifi."

Jack didn't look amused. "There is no balcony."

Good point.

"So, what's your new idea?"

"I've made a drawing." He pointed to a brown paper bag on the bed, on which some child had scribbled lines with crayon.

The doorbell rang.

"C'mon in." Jack's shout echoed through the nearly empty apartment.

I gave him one of those looks. You know, the kind that said, Are you nuts? This is New York City. You could be inviting a serial killer inside.

No serial killers, just Neil and (surprise) his son David,

who would be project foreman. Before I could make the introductions, David kissed me lightly on the cheek. Something he'd never done in the more than a dozen years I've known him.

Achilles growled.

And, I'm positive, Jack did, too.

For the next hour, I kept myself strategically placed between the two younger men. I wanted the contractor and the client to be on the same side. I was thinking deadline, budget and referrals, not possible hand-to-hand combat over my body.

Neil and David loved the apartment, especially the two wood-burning fireplaces, although we talked about the possibility of one huge fireplace. There was a brief intermission in the tour—and discussion—while the three he-men showed each other that the wood-burning fireplaces worked. In lieu of wood, several sections of that day's *Times* proved invaluable in the demonstration. Once the he-men remembered to open the dampers.

I had the right answers to all of Neil's budget questions.

They gave a thumbs-up to my design plans (the second kitchen-turned-study got raves).

They agreed that altering the living room windows would be a major problem and major expense, but hey, if that's what Jack wanted and the co-op board approved, they'd do it.

Jack never mentioned his design idea. And I didn't ask.

All in all, a good meeting. By the time Neil and David left, the trio had completed male bonding. David's buss to my cheek was apparently forgiven and/or forgotten. One never knew with men. It didn't hurt that Neil and David were longtime fans of *The D.A. Chronicles.*

Once they were out the door, Jack turned to me. "Let's grab lunch."

"I should get home and start working on those revised bedroom plans."

"What happened to not working weekends?"

He would pick up on that. "I really need to talk to David."

"What's with David? You two an item?"

"You jealous?" Evidently, David kissing me had, in fact, left an impression.

Jack rolled his eyes. "Nah. It's just that you haven't dated in…a while. So if you want to date David, well, that's a good sign. That you're in recovery."

"Don't go there, Jack."

Of course, maybe if Jack-the-best-friend had "gone there" more enthusiastically, I might not have ended up *with*, and then *without*, Trey. And subsequently tumbled into bed with my Big Mistake.

Destiny or downfall. Vanessa the psychic didn't leave me much of a choice.

"Just trying to be helpful." Pause. "You look like you could use…lunch."

"I'm fine." Then my stomach growled, betraying me once more. Sigh. I agreed only because it was easier than arguing (Vanessa, again). And it was only lunch, not a lifetime commitment. "Somewhere in the neighborhood. It has to be quick."

"Let's walk up to Ninety-sixth." When Jack said *walk*, Achilles bounded over, gripping the leash between his teeth.

"No dog." I was adamant. "No Spencer's Deli. It's your treat. I want a real lunch and I get to choose the place."

No reason not to choose the most expensive, and the most popular, Italian pizza palace on the Upper West Side. Which did not take reservations. As I'd expected, the line flowed like a rushing river out the door.

Jack jabbed my shoulder. "Give your name to the hostess."

"You forgot yours?"

"No." On went the mirrored sunglasses, followed by a baseball cap he'd whipped out of his back pocket. "I just don't want to be recognized."

As I waited for the hostess to take my name, I observed a group of teenage girls who'd started giggling, and soon the news spread loudly that the sexy and rakish Logan Hunter was here for pizza.

Most native New Yorkers were blasé when they saw celebs on the street, walking through the shops or dining in restaurants. But sometimes—and it looked like this was going to be one of those times—tourists tended to get a bit overenthusiastic.

"Sullivan. For two," I told the hostess over the sound of rising giggles.

"Forty-five minutes," she told me.

I nodded glumly. Forty-five minutes longer than I wanted to spend in public with Jack Spencer. I turned and searched for Jack in the swelling crowd. By the time I got back to our spot in line, he was surrounded.

First, by the group of teenage girls. The one who looked like the leader of the pack whispered something in Jack's ear that turned his face a pale shade of red. But I heard the part that included "...and a tattoo you'd never guess where." I'd never seen Jack blush. Kinda cute.

Then came the tourist-style paparazzi, who begged him to pose for pictures. (First, a large group photo, then, individual shots with Jack's arm draped around each bright-eyed fan's shoulders. I counted twenty.)

Through it all, Jack teased the fans, joked with them. Answered questions strangers shouldn't ask, but did because they felt an unexplained closeness to a celebrity they didn't really know. I had to smile when Jack blushed again, when a lovely woman old enough to be his mother kissed him soundly on the lips and pinched him on the ass.

This was a role I'd never seen Jack play. The man who'd once been my best friend was a TV sex symbol. I hardly recognized him. He looked the same, but he was different. The Jack Spencer standing next to me was a complete stranger. And one I wasn't sure I was ready to meet (or have lunch with).

So much had changed, not only in our lives, but between us. And I couldn't put aside this feeling our relationship wasn't going to be the same again.

I knew we needed to talk. About that night we had sex. About our friendship. About what happened next.

But where to begin?

Jack grabbed my arm, hustled me to the front of the line. "Spencer, for two, somewhere inside that's private and quiet."

The bright-eyed hostess (she immediately recognized Jack and reminded him they'd once worked in an off-off-Broadway show together) promptly found us an empty table for four, right in the center of the restaurant. So much for private and quiet.

She handed us menus and hovered at Jack's side, waiting for us to order. (Large pepperoni pizza, extra cheese, two antipastos, a glass of merlot for Jack and diet soda for me.)

The wine and Diet Coke arrived quickly, and Jack picked up his glass and touched it to mine. "To new beginnings."

"What's that supposed to mean?"

He shrugged. "Just that you seem to be moving on in your life. So if you're not dating David, who are you dating?"

"The woman you're seeing...*seriously*?"

"That's not your question. You want to know if I'm sleeping with Sheli."

"No." Yes.

"You first. Sleeping with David?"

"That's none of your business."

He settled back into his chair and studied me. "I miss the Megan Sullivan who used to tell me everything."

"That was Before."

"Before what?"

"Before we slept together."

Complete silence.

"That's it?" I asked. "No explanation? No apology? Not even an 'I'm sorry we had sex. And ruined everything'?"

He'd just taken a sip of wine and was having a difficult time deciding whether to swallow, or spit it out. He swallowed, hard, and with a surprisingly shaky hand put the glass down. "I don't know what…just that…you were…I wasn't thinking clearly…it just happened."

Jack was rambling, fumbling, and doing both badly. Guess he didn't work well these days without a script in front of him. He leaned over and asked quietly, "You really want to have this conversation now, here?"

"Yes." No.

"I'd never hurt you. Never meant to hurt you. Cross my heart." Which he did. "But I never got a chance to tell you, because you disappeared without a word."

"And if I'd stayed?"

Significant pause. He looked me straight in the eye. "We'll never know, will we?"

We sat there, watching each other warily.

Okay, so this wasn't exactly the road I'd envisioned our conversation taking. Even though I was doing a pretty good job of it, I wasn't comfortable at playing the shrew. And I didn't want to spend the rest of my life angry with Jack.

What I wanted was for everything to go back to Before. But I never got the chance to say that because...

"Jack, darling..."

I glanced up to see a slender brunette, size minus-zero, standing behind Jack. She wrapped her arms around his chest while she nuzzled first his right ear then his left.

Jack struggled, not hard enough in my opinion, to wiggle out of her embrace. "Megan, this is Jeri."

"Jeri with a *j*, one *r* and an *i*. I'm a model and an actress." She slid into an empty chair, keeping her gaze on Jack and ignoring me. Maybe she thought that would make me go away.

Before she'd arrived, I'd have given anything to disappear. But now, no way. I was curious to see one of America's Sexiest Men Alive in action.

At Jack's introduction, her catlike eyes shifted slightly in my direction, but she kept her radar totally focused on him. "We've missed you."

I won't bore you with the blather (from both of them) that followed. They talked around me, through me, but never to me. Suffice to say that after a few minutes, I couldn't take it much longer without doing some bodily harm to the surgically enhanced Jeri with a *j*, one *r* and an *i*.

The pizza and antipasto arrived on cue, but I'd lost my appetite. Whatever had made me think I could, or should, fix whatever was broken between me and Jack? I excused myself to go to the ladies' room. I brushed by Jack and seriously considered wrapping my arms around his chest and biting his ear. Why should the model-slash-actress be the only one to leave her imprint on Jack Spencer?

But I restrained myself. After I locked myself in the last

empty stall in the women's room, I pulled out my cell phone and called Chloe.

"Whatever you're doing, get over to Giorgio's now!"

"I'm painting my toenails."

I explained the situation. "I need you to save me from myself. And a possible murder-one conviction." Then hung up before she could ask the name of my intended victim(s).

When I stepped out of the women's room, I felt a bit disoriented because I couldn't find Jack or our table.

But there was a crowd surrounding the spot where I thought our table was located. I pushed my way through to find Jack surrounded by fans clamoring for autographs, and a TV crew from *Undercover Hollywood* trying to get the best angles. Jeri was posing for pictures for the paparazzi. And in my chair sat the gossip columnist from one of the city's notorious tabloids. Propped up next to her was a woman I learned later was the publicist from Jack's TV show.

Everyone fawned all over Jack. And he seemed to be enjoying the attention. Finally, he glanced up and caught my eye.

"I have to go," I told him. Easier said than done. It took a few minutes and several well-placed elbows into strangers before I could make it through the crowd and to the exit.

But, like Lot's wife, I couldn't help myself, and slowly turned around to see the destruction. Then I was out the door and halfway down the street before I felt a tug on my shoulder.

"Megan, wait. You can't honestly think I encouraged that."

I picked up my pace. "You didn't discourage it."

Jack yanked my arm. It was either stop, or lose the limb.

"It's part of my *job*. I didn't plan it. The studio publicist was having lunch with the woman from the *Post*. I couldn't be rude." Pause. "*You* picked the restaurant."

"Leave me alone." Something in my tone of voice—I heard the defeat as well as the weariness—must have convinced him I was serious.

"All right. If that's what you really want." His hand slid from my shoulder.

I started walking. He didn't follow.

That hurt more than I can tell you.

When I got to the corner, I turned and saw Jack standing in front of the restaurant, chatting with a bunch of women.

I punched out Chloe's number on my cell, updated her about the near-riot at Giorgio's, and quickly walked the twenty blocks to her apartment on Seventy-second and Amsterdam. She perched on her front stoop, a diet cola in one hand, a beer in the other. I knew which one I wanted, but accepted the cola because last New Year's Day I'd vowed never to get drunk over Jack Spencer again.

"I made a mess of it."

With a dramatic flourish, Chloe produced two spoons and a four-inch, square, white cake box, and we began to pay homage to a large piece of tiramisu.

"You claim you're not interested in Jack personally, emotionally or intimately," Chloe pointed out. "So why are you upset when other women, like this Jeri with a *j*, one *r* and an *i*, find him sexy and desirable? Or when he might find them sexy and desirable?"

Finally, a question I could answer. "I miss him. I want my best friend back. I'm attracted to him. I don't want to be, but I am. That scares me. After being with Jack, I don't want to have sex with anyone else. But sex with Jack isn't

going to happen again, and if I'm celibate, I'm never going
to have a Great Love of My Life. Because the Great Love
of My Life is going to want to have sex with me. A lot."

"Step one."

I grabbed her spoon. "What are you talking about?"

"Admitting you're addicted."

"You're saying I need professional help to get over Jack."

"Yes," Chloe said solemnly, "you do."

Now my business partner thought I should see a shrink.
What would she say/do when/if I admitted to visiting a
psychic?

"But why pay a shrink when you have girlfriends?"
Chloe made a few calls on her cell, and within minutes had
arranged a Saturday Girl's Night Only party.

The ingredients:

Me, the one who's addicted; Chloe, the rational one;
and three other women—Kim, a mutual friend who'd just
gotten married; Sara, Chloe's neighbor and a doctoral can-
didate in psychology; and Liz, a divorce lawyer (in the
middle of a divorce) who Chloe met in yoga class.

Mix, stir and—voilà!—you've got an instant women's
support group. Worked for me.

Chloe sent me home to get ready for the evening. "Indulge in a bubble bath. Take a nap. Expect us at seven."

"What about food? Drinks?" I've been well-trained by
both Ritas in the art of being a perfect hostess.

She stared at me long and hard. "I'll handle the refresh-
ments. Just relax. We're gonna help you figure out Jack and
then what to do about him."

I took the Number One subway down to The Village,
played with and fed the cat—who'd been feeling so neglected that she let me cuddle her for a full minute—tossed
a load of laundry in the community washer and remem-

bered to check my answering machine. The message light flashed four times.

My mother: Please, Megan, don't forget the cheesecake! My sisters.

First, Patty: I've changed my mind. I do want to wallpaper the kids' bath. Call me.

Then Ellyn: Just FYI, you owe me twenty-five bucks for your share of Patty's birthday present. We're celebrating tomorrow. Don't forget the cheesecake. Cherry. No, blueberry. Get both.

Followed by a mysterious caller who invited me to invest in my future for as little as five thousand dollars down. Right.

No call of apology from Jack. Well, what did I expect? I'd told him to leave me alone. I'd left him with my uneaten pizza in the clutches of dozens of model-like women, a restaurant hostess and several waitresses who'd probably toss their day's tips for a chance to be tossed by Jack.

Chloe was right. I did need help. Desperately.

Despite the order not to worry about feeding my guests, I ran over to the corner supermarket, invested in a two-liter bottle of diet soda, a bottle of red wine, a package of raw cashews and a bag of Oreos (double filling). I grabbed a cab and went over to the Chelsea Spencer's and picked up two blueberry cheesecakes. And asked them to set aside another blueberry and a cherry for pickup tomorrow.

When I got home, I changed clothes and figured I had about forty minutes left to straighten up the place.

I'd lived in this studio apartment in The Village since I'd graduated from the Rhode Island School of Design. At close to a thousand bucks per month, I was paying more than two bucks a square foot, but in Manhattan, it's all about location, location, location. Plus, I had French doors that doubled as my front windows and led out to a tiny balcony overlooking Minetta Lane.

It's a great street, just a few blocks from Washington Square. I had terrific next-door neighbors (on the left, a couple who taught at NYU; across the hall, a flautist with the New York Philharmonic; and downstairs, an artist who had a studio in Long Island City, and who watched the cat whenever I was away). They'd all been living here years longer than me.

Like many interior designers, my apartment tended to either temporarily take on the look of the client I was working with, or be a mishmash of styles that were the "me" of the moment.

Currently, I was living with an eclectic mix of vintage furniture and vibrant fabric, which included a deep red leather ottoman recently thrown in for effect. My color for the week was blue, one of the accent colors I'd been considering for Jack's apartment. There was every shade you could imagine, from the midnight-blue area rug covering the hardwood floor to the palest of blue pieces of silk fabric draping the French doors.

Which is what greeted the women when they arrived en masse shortly after seven.

Since I had no idea how a group like this functioned, I figured it would be smart to listen to what the other women had to say before offering my support or begging for theirs.

We pulled huge, fluffy sapphire pillows from a stack in the corner to in front of the fireplace, where the mantel was faux-painted a cornflower blue. (Something I wouldn't do at Jack's, but right now I liked the look for me.) Chloe put on some light jazz CDs, and we lit aromatherapy candles (blue for the sky), poured glasses of wine (diet soda for me so I could keep a clear head) and went around the room, sharing our stories of romantic flings and failures.

The highlights:

Kim (recently married): I never thought I would say this. I'm getting too much sex.

*Collective gasp. We all wanted to know her secret.*

Sara (the almost Ph. D.): You all keep telling me what you're thinking. But how do you really feel?

*We bombarded her with (blue) pillows from the (blue) slip-covered couch.*

Liz (the divorce lawyer in the middle of a divorce): He cheated from the moment I met him.

*We all agreed, he's gonna cheat on the "other woman," too. If she doesn't cheat on him first.*

Chloe (the rational one): I understand that a man can be married to one woman at a time. Today he's married to his job. I can accept that.

*She's a bitch. And she'll turn on him, we told her, as soon as the stock market dipped.*

Then it was my turn.

"My name is Megan Sullivan, and I am—" I looked to Chloe for guidance and continued, following her nod of encouragement "—addicted to Jack Spencer."

From the reaction, you'd have thought Chloe had assembled the Greenwich Village chapter of the Jack Spencer Fan Club.

Me: And I need your help.

Liz: Details! We need details!

Sara: But how do you feel?

Liz: One word. Hunk.

Sara: But how do you feel?

Kim: Is he good in bed?

Chloe: Settle down ladies. Maybe Megan should start

at the beginning. (Said in an encouraging, if somewhat placating, tone of voice, because I was about to bolt and she knew it.)

The ladies settled, with their glasses topped off and second helpings of blueberry cheesecake in hand.

"What's said here, stays here," Chloe warned in her nice but take-charge voice. "I mean it. No Page Six. No *Extra*. If I hear or read anything about what's said here tonight, I will hunt you down and…" She sliced her finger under and across her neck.

"They get your point," I said dryly.

I finished my piece of cheesecake and started another before beginning my story. I told them about the naked baby picture, about that first kiss at sixteen on the co-op's rooftop. About how important my friendship with Jack had been.

I told them about meeting my ex-fiancé and learning he'd eloped with the wedding planner. About how alone I felt on New Year's Eve, and how I ended up having rooftop sex with Jack. And then I offered a brief history of our current involvement, including today's episode at the restaurant.

"So you can see," I wrapped up my story, "I need help."

These women sat there, silently, looking at me as though I was absolutely crazy.

I looked to Chloe for a clue.

"Any suggestions or advice for Megan?" Chloe asked.

There were no takers.

Had I stumped them all?

Was I—and my situation, dare I say it, my addiction— hopeless and without possibility of a cure?

I looked at Liz. She shrugged. "I'd sleep with him again."

Then over to Kim. "Sorry. If I was ever considering cheating on Alex, it would be with Jack Spencer."

I turned to Sara. "Don't," I begged, "ask me how I feel."

I knew Chloe really thought these women could help me figure out, even get over, Jack Spencer. Or deal with my feelings for him in a way that wouldn't get me arrested or mentioned in the gossip tabs.

They'd done their best, I guess. So I did what any good hostess did in an awkward situation. I brought out the second cheesecake. It went very well with the bottle of champagne Chloe dashed out to buy.

It was nearly eleven when I poured the quartet into a taxi. They were feeling no pain. I was feeling depressed.

I went upstairs to clean up the mess in the apartment.

The mess in my life would take a lot more work.

I dumped the dishes in the tiny sink. And wrapped up the last few crumbs of cheesecake. And noticed that there were two new messages on the answering machine.

I poured what remained of the champagne (about a shot glass full) into a mug, poured myself onto my Bentwood rocking chair and wrapped the chenille throw around me. Emma climbed onto my lap and cuddled up, purred and went to sleep.

I sipped the champagne and pressed the button on the answering machine.

My mother: You won't forget the cheesecake.

No ma'am. I won't.

The tears welled in my eyes. Over cheesecake? Well, at least my mother cared enough to call and remind me.

It was the voice on the second call that got my attention.

"Hello. Is this Megan Sullivan's machine?" Pause. "This is Vanessa, your psychic. I feel your ambivalence, dear. But, trust me, he is worth shedding tears over. It can never be the same, dear. But it can be better. Good night."

Click. I hit the save button. And let those tears fall.

# 6

*Jack*

DON'T BELIEVE WHAT YOU read about me in the gossip rags.

I'm not the tough, arrogant, always-in-control, lives-for-and-in-the-fast-lane, brooding and mysterious guy I play on *The D.A. Chronicles*. I'm as perplexed about life and love—and how to make the most of both—as most of you.

And I'm still reeling from the Restaurant Episode. I guess I mishandled the situation. Although I'm still hazy about what actually happened that caused Megan to storm out, I'm sure I'll read all the details—courtesy of a certain see-all, tell-all gossip columnist.

What did come through loud and clear, however, was that after all our years of friendship, everything we'd gone through together, Megan was unable to separate the reel me from the real me. And that hurt more than I can tell you.

My friend and colleague, Sam Davies, thought the real me needed to morph from Nice Guy into Tough Guy.

And he told me so (on Friday night, as we were both dateless). "It'll blast your 'Q Factor' into the stratosphere," he said, as we shot hoops in the health club's basketball court. "And I guarantee you'll impress the woman you want to impress."

"That's Sheli," I said with feeling, as much to convince him as myself. Then I watched as the ball swirled around the rim before dropping to the court—outside the basket for the third time. It looked as though my dating techniques weren't the only skills that needed improvement.

"That's Megan." Sam sadly shook his head. "No crime asking for professional help. Which you need. Badly."

I shrugged. "I can figure this out for myself." Of course I could!

"Or," Sam said thoughtfully, "you can ask Rachel and Alicia."

"The costume czarina and my makeup goddess?" I tried to keep the terror out of my voice. Failed. The two of them? Offering advice? To me? I froze in place, long enough for Sam to grab the ball.

"Not. To. Worry," Sam said between dribbles. He aimed for the basket and scored another two points. "They're already working up a plan."

"What…kind…of plan?" I let the basketball bounce past me. Don't get me wrong, I got along well with Rachel and Alicia. I'd let them dress me in tweed and/or plaid and paint my face red with purple stripes if the script called for it. But I wasn't about to turn my love life over to a pair of twenty-somethings who, well…I wasn't going anywhere near there willingly.

"It's less of a plan and more of an improvisation."

And that's all he would say, even though I threatened bodily harm.

"Introduce me to Gerry, one of the Style Guys you've been blathering on about," I pleaded. Gerry and his two gay pals have this weekly fashion show for women on Cable Z. Maybe they'd see me as a challenge, take me on and make me over.

"No can do. We broke up."

"Sorry." I really was. "Then I'll have to rent that Mel Gibson chick flick. Again."

That's the one where he was zapped by electricity and read Helen Hunt's mind, only to discover that reading women's minds can be hazardous to a man's sanity.

"I don't see why asking Alicia and Rachel for help is a problem," Sam said. "They *like* you. They *want* to help you."

"They like Megan," I corrected. I remembered exactly what the two women had said to me after lunch at The Cloisters. "You are so not worthy," and, "We have the power to fix him," don't exactly inspire confidence in their abilities to see beyond my XY chromosomes. "I'll think about it."

"Don't think too long." Pause. "Megan's gonna start dating soon."

"That would be best for her," I said evenly. But I was thinking, why was everyone around me so interested in my (lack of) love life? Specifically as that love life applied to Megan Sullivan. I didn't want to picture the costume czarina and makeup goddess as Ritas-in-training. The thought was not only mind-boggling, it sent shivers of fear racing through my body.

I had to sit down. "Maybe you and Gerry will get back together."

"Not likely." Sam joined me on the gym bleachers. "Hey, these things happen." (Translation: Why do they always happen to you and me?)

"Tell you what," I conceded. "I'll agree to *think* about being subjected to a Rachel-Alicia makeover if you go through it with me."

The look on Sam's face was priceless. Turning the tables got 'em every time.

"Let me get back to you on that," he said with an equal mixture of grudge and admiration.

"Deal." We shook hands and began another round of hoops.

I wasn't convinced that Sam's suggestion to put myself in the hands of a pair of amateurs would pay off, but I was willing to consider—that's consider, not commit to—almost anything.

Because, you see, after much soul-searching, I figured out I'd blown it big-time with Megan. That look on her face when she left the restaurant—pale, weary, defeated, so totally *not* the Megan Sullivan I knew and, yes, admired—will haunt me forever.

So while I let Sam's out-of-the-box idea (Rachel-Alicia) percolate, I worked on what I would say to Megan. Because, deep in my soul I would always be a Nice Guy (understanding and humble) even as I was transforming myself into a Tough Guy.

If I believed (or wanted to believe) that Megan was jealous over the attention paid me by a wannabe model I barely knew, that meant she still cared about me. Even if just a little.

"Or," I told Achilles on Sunday morning as I snapped on his leash and we bounded down the stairs, because he was now refusing to ride the elevator, "I am deluding myself."

It was a beautiful summer morning, just before nine. Sunny, no clouds, with a touch of breeze off the Hudson. My dog raced for the corner newsstand and dragged me along with him. I picked up a copy of the *Times*, and we meandered along Broadway until we hit the Spencer's at Ninety-sixth Street. I parked the dog at one of the tables outside and went inside to pick up breakfast.

The deli hadn't changed in the weeks since my parents had moved to Florida, but it felt strange not to have my dad at the counter, slapping cream cheese on bagels and shouting hello to his regular customers.

The ageless Sol Hersch, a family friend my dad lured out of semiretirement to oversee the three Spencer's, had a bialy with the works and a large black coffee waiting for me. Even when I'd been living downtown in Chelsea, I'd still come uptown for Sunday breakfast. Yes, I was a creature of habit.

"So Mr. TV Star," Sol called out so everyone in the deli and the surrounding ten-block area could hear, "how you like living back in the old neighborhood?"

"The old neighborhood's just fine." The bialy was warm. The coffee, hot as Hades. A good start to the day.

"I hear you're going to modernize. Put some—" Sol raised his fisted hands into the air like a boxer "—pep into the old place."

"Gonna try. You'll come by often and let me know how I'm doing."

Sol's laughter followed me outside. Achilles was happily gnawing on one of the chew toys I'd brought along. I settled into my chair, opened the *Times* to the Arts & Leisure section and started reading about what the theater world was up to.

"If you look at the bottom left-hand corner, Jack," a sexy voice whispered from across my table, "I guarantee you won't be disappointed."

I recognized the voice. And the face of the striking-looking woman who'd slid into the empty chair. Fellow NYU'er Phoebe Silverstone, blond and elfin, pointed to the article she was talking about.

The first paragraph said it all. "Phoebe Silverstone takes a starring role in a new off-Broadway play by (insert name of famous Pulitzer prize-winning playwright here). On Theater Row." I looked up at her. "Very impressive. Congrats."

"Thanks." Longtime acquaintances that we were (I'm

godfather to her year-old baby boy) she had no qualms about nibbling on the corner of my bialy. "Are you interested?"

"Sure. Invite me to opening night. I'll be there cheering for you."

"Not in the audience. Up on stage. With me."

She named an actor whose lengthy résumé I knew. "Left us high and dry yesterday, right in the middle of rehearsals." She sighed. "He took some silly cable TV Movie of the Week in Hollywood."

"Talk about coincidences," I deadpanned. "I just turned down a silly cable TV Movie of the Week in Hollywood."

She laughed. "I suggested your name to the director. He's a big fan of your show. I think he directed an episode or two. He was supposed to get in touch with your agent."

My hard-working agent, who'd likely left a message on my cell, since I hadn't gotten around to transferring my phone service up to the new place. "We go on hiatus end of next week," I said. "If I can make it work, I'd love to do it."

Phoebe hefted onto the table a beaded bag large enough for her to crawl into, and pulled out a bound copy of the play. "Let me know what you think."

"How did you know I'd be here this morning?"

She rolled her eyes. "Jack, Jack, Jack. Sunday mornings. Spencer's. Bialy and coffee. Sunday *Times*." Dramatic pause. "You might want to read today's gossip column in your favorite tabloid."

I have to tell you, my heart stopped. I swear, for a full minute. "Don't go anywhere," I ordered hoarsely when it started beating again.

Calmly (well, not as calmly as I'd have liked) I stepped inside the deli and rustled through the stack of newspapers until I found a copy of the *New York Ledger.*

This kind of reading needed to be done sitting down.

So I did, and slowly turned the pages until I found the column. There it was, a mere inch or so of type about me, all names boldfaced, and I could hear the words being shouted as I read them silently.

In case you missed it:

"TV heartthrob Jack Spencer (Logan Hunter on *The D.A. Chronicles*) is juggling several new loves in his life: a co-op near the river on the Upper West Side and a leggy redhead—name unknown. We hear she's renovating Jack's home as well as his you know what (wink, wink). There's a petite brunette from La La Land who's relocating, as well. To Jack's new apartment?"

Dammit! Talk about embarrassing. I'd come to accept that negative publicity comes with the territory I'd been walking. This was a bit off the mark (Sheli moving into the co-op), but also a little too close to the truth. Was it too much to hope Megan hadn't read this thing?

I ripped out the page, crumpled it into a ball and made a perfect three-point toss into the trash can by the door.

"Wanna talk about it?" Phoebe asked, as she polished off the rest of my bialy and started in on the coffee.

Which was okay, since I no longer had an appetite.

Did I want to talk about it? "I could use a woman's perspective," I admitted reluctantly. I'd skimmed through enough of the women's magazines to know that the advice they offered was so complicated (and convoluted) that those of us with XY chromosomes needed either a Ph.D. or a trusted XX-chromosome person to decipher some of the code.

I'd met Phoebe at NYU. On the first day of Acting 101, we were plucked out of student obscurity and paired to give a cold reading in front of our classmates (all strangers, and not unlike facing a real-life audience).

We'd barely made it to the end of the scene before both of us dashed out of the theater space and tossed our cookies in the respective men's and women's rooms.

You'll be relieved to learn I've gotten much better at auditioning.

I outlined the highlights (or lowlights), sparing Phoebe the backstory because she'd met Megan many times over the years. "That night was pure chemistry. Then, on the morning after the best sex a man could hope for, she disappeared without a word."

Phoebe nodded. "I can see where she's coming from. She thought it was pity sex."

"Pity sex." I slowly repeated the words. "As in, I stepped into an unmarked minefield and something exploded, but it's my fault for not knowing there was a minefield there?"

Phoebe leaned back and gave me one of *those* looks.

Wait a minute. Phoebe's supposed to be on my side. Which was what I told her.

"There are no sides here," Phoebe explained patiently. "There's your perception. And there's Megan's. You know Jack, this is the conversation you should be having with her."

I knew that. Of course I did. "Thanks," I muttered, not feeling exactly thankful. "For the advice. And for the job op."

"But I have a question you need to answer quickly before you have time to think about it," Phoebe said as she got up to leave. "Why is it so important to make a clean break with Megan, who you say you don't have romantic feelings for, in order to start a romantic relationship with another woman? Do you need Megan's approval? Or do you need something more?"

Don't you hate trick questions? Or ones without multiple choice answers?

I mumbled some nonsensical answer, gave Phoebe a

hug and slumped back in my chair, then dug out my cell and checked for messages.

That, at least, would allow me to procrastinate and not consider Phoebe's very astute observation.

Which woman I really wanted in my life.

Yep. One call from my agent. The director of Phoebe's play wanted a meet this morning at eleven. Doable. I gathered up the script, the *Times* and the dog, and headed home. A quick shower, a change into fresh clothes and I was on my way to Theater Row on Forty-second Street.

By noon, I'd read a few scenes and knew I'd scored the part, and that a formal offer would be made later that afternoon. *The D.A. Chronicles* would wrap for the season at the end of this week, and I'd start play rehearsals on Tuesday. We'd open mid-July for a limited, six-week run. I'd get a week's vacation before heading back to TV Land, assuming my character wasn't found dead tomorrow morning up at The Cloisters. (Still waiting for pages forty-seven through fifty-two.)

Career in high gear. Personal life spread all over the gossip tabs for the world-at-large to read.

A WEEK HAD PASSED SINCE I'd spoken with Megan. Would she take my call? Or hang up when she heard my voice? Or maybe I should just drop by. A casual I'm-just-in-the-neighborhood kind of drop by. She might refuse to open her door. But that was a chance I had to take.

I hopped on the Broadway local and made it as far as Chelsea before I got cold feet. I get enough rejection in my professional life that I wasn't up to more rejection in my personal life.

I dashed off the subway at Twenty-third Street and Broadway, and headed to Spencer's and some cheesecake.

But who should I see coming out of Spencer's, two boxed cheesecakes in hand? You guessed right.

Megan.

So I followed her down the street, using the tracking skills I'd developed as hotshot A.D.A. Logan Hunter. She walked toward the subway station at Fourteenth Street, no doubt headed for New Jersey and dinner with her family. I could sorta casually saunter up to her on the subway platform and maybe wheedle an invite.

She paused briefly at a storefront window, forcing me to hide behind a street pole. When she continued walking, I hesitated a bit before following. I jogged over to the spot where she'd stopped, and stared at the neon sign in the window. Vanessa the Psychic. Now what was that all about?

I caught sight of Megan as she disappeared down the subway steps, and I picked up my pace. I didn't want to miss the next train. I found her standing on the platform.

"You lost?" she asked, in what I was supposed to believe was a bored, totally uninterested, tone of voice.

"You gonna make it to NJ in time for dinner?"

Megan rolled her eyes in response.

"I'm sorry," I said.

At the same time, Megan said, "Don't apologize. Because if you do I'll feel obligated to accept it, and I'm not ready to."

I'm trying to see where she's coming from.

"You'd think," I said carefully, so as not to upset the delicate balance here, "that two intelligent people could talk out their differences and figure a way to get past them. Especially since they're working on a project that's gonna throw them in each other's paths for the next couple of months."

I could tell she was mentally dissecting my words and trying hard to find the flaw in my statement.

"Unless," Megan said softly, "the more intelligent of the two decides to pull out because of artistic differences."

"To which," I replied, "she might find herself and her fledgling company sued. Which would benefit neither party."

The conversation took a break as the subway roared into the station. She got on the train. I followed.

"Would you agree," Megan asked as we bumped along, "that we've turned into two cranky, stubborn people who tend to bring out the worst in each other?"

"That about sums us up." Now that we were talking, I wasn't sure what to say. "I'd like to answer that question. You know, the one…"

"Can I beg a favor?" she continued before I could say another word. "Don't answer. I'm sure your response would be illuminating, perhaps entertaining, but I'm even more sure it would piss me off."

Nodding slowly, I said, "I can do that."

"Good. You know how I tend to procrastinate in coming up with New Year's resolutions? This year's will be to forget last New Year's Eve. Actually, I resolve to forget everything I did, or said, between Christmas and New Year's Day."

Talk about surprises. Megan had, in effect, absolved me of my sin(s) because, in her view, they never happened.

Wait a minute. I can't forget. I don't want to forget. And I sure as hell don't want her to forget. Which, of course, made absolutely no sense, since I want to move on.

Which led me back to Phoebe's questions.

Why was it so important for me to set things straight with Megan? To discuss one night of physical intimacy that wasn't going to happen again in my lifetime because Megan considered me pond scum?

To apologize for what happened at Giorgio's? To put our friendship back on track, that's for sure. Although I wasn't sure we could do it, considering how badly we'd messed up. (Hey, I wasn't the only one to blame here. It takes two people to make or break a relationship/friendship.) But I was gonna try.

"Don't you think we'd both be better off if we talked about it? Resolved it?"

"You will do this for me, Jack." She glared at me. "I don't want to get involved with you. *That* way. We come together, like at the restaurant, and just clash, and it's exhausting and I can't take it anymore. I'm not going to cry my eyes out over you ever again."

I know about the exhausting bit. Wait. She just admitted she'd cried over me.

"We need to keep it…professional," she said with a bit of a hitch to her voice that told me perhaps Megan wasn't as sure about this as she wanted to sound. "The apartment renovation comes first. That's business."

"What about our friendship?"

She shook her head.

"We're not friends?" Now I was confused. "I've known you forever. If we're not friends, what happened?"

"We had sex."

It figures. Sex had become, between me and Megan, both a conversation- and a friendship-killer.

The subway pulled into Penn Station at Thirty-fourth Street and Megan got off. No invite to join her, so I did the only thing I could. I rode back uptown.

Several hours later, as I sat on my front stoop, beer in hand, I was still trying to decipher that entire conversation.

Including her parting shot before the subway doors closed: "I'm happy for you. About Sheli, I mean."

I was spittin' angry that Megan could reduce the past thirty years of our lives to "we had sex." Followed by, "I'm happy for you."

Forget the good times.

Forget the friendship that we'd shared.

Forget it all.

Wasn't it convenient that neither of us wanted to get together?

I slept badly that night. I'd gotten exactly what I thought I wanted, so I should have slept like a baby. But I didn't. Which meant I was a lot cranky when Sexy Voice's wake-up call came at four o'clock Friday morning. I was at The Cloisters by six to film the final scenes of the season-ending cliff-hanger.

We'd finally been blessed with pages forty-seven through fifty-two. Actually, three versions of the final scenes.

In version one, Caitlin was shot.

In version two, I got it in the back.

In version three, bang! bang! for us both.

But I wouldn't know which version the network chose until I watched the season premiere come fall. Then we shot three different openings for resolution of the cliff-hanger.

In version one, Caitlin died.

In version two, I died.

In version three, we both died.

By the time we wrapped at seven p.m., I was wiped.

And had a few months ahead of me before I had to start worrying about whether there'd be another season of *The D.A. Chronicles* in my future.

Meanwhile, I had this summer job, in an off-Broadway play. Nice paycheck. Short rehearsal time. Eight performances a week.

And several days off before I had to report for rehearsals.

Sam was still in a funk over his falling-out with Gerry. He was heading immediately to his little oceanfront cottage in the Hamptons where he'd spend the summer, and he'd invited me (and Achilles) to join him for the weekend. All I needed to bring, he suggested, was some additional "reading" material.

Lots of sun. Long stretches of sand. No stress.

Sounded better than good to me.

So I packed my bag and rented a car, and soon Achilles and I began the two-hour drive eastbound on the LIE (that's Long Island Expressway) to the far end of Long Island, away from renovation projects that included my co-op apartment and my relationship with Megan.

Sam met me at the door with a beer in hand. "Did you bring the women's mags so we can prep?"

"You're in this with me?"

He sucked in a deep breath. "Yeah."

I'd bought a few new ones so I could keep current on the ways of women. "Most of the advice is pure garbage."

"Someone's believing it, or these magazines wouldn't be flying off the shelves," he said.

"But are the magazines telling women what us men really want? Or what we say we want, because that's what women want to hear?"

"Get a clue, Jack. It's what women want to hear."

We hunkered down on the futon. Sam opened one of the magazines and turned to the first page I'd earmarked.

"We're gonna take a little quiz, so put yourself in—whose mind, Megan's or Sheli's?—when answering."

I started to say Sheli, but Megan's name popped out.

He cocked a brow. "Here's ten questions to determine your compatibility in and out of bed," he started to read.

"Score your lover from one to five. Rate the first time the two of you had sex."

"She's rating *me?*"

He nodded.

Heavy sigh. "My ego says ten." Yeah, yeah—the quiz says a five is tops. But I expected I'd need those extra points.

"Then ten it is. Number two. How breathless does his kiss makes you feel?"

Do I count when Megan and I were sixteen, and practically collapsed with laughter after locking lips? Or New Year's Eve before we did It? Or the night I drove her home from New Jersey? "I'd have to say five."

"Question three. How often does he send you conflicting messages?"

"What kind of conflicting messages?"

Sam shoved the magazine in front of my face. "I'm reading the questions, not interpreting them. Wanna pass on that one?"

"Let's pass on the quiz," I suggested. "What else?"

He thumbed through the pages. "Here's an article that asks, 'Think Being a Guy is Easy?'"

"Let me see that." I took the magazine. "It takes a full two pages to answer 'no'?"

Sam shrugged. He skimmed the article. "I'll save you the trouble of reading. Everything has to do with the mighty penis."

"I think they're more obsessed with it than we are." I picked up another magazine and read the cover headlines: "Who's Your Best Love Match?"; "Sex: The Number One Secret You Have to Know"; "Men: What They Really Think is Sexy." The magazine slid to the floor. "It's all about sex. There's nothing here about building relationships."

"And that's because sex," Sam said sagely, "is exactly what women think all men want all the time."

Sad, isn't it? Because despite what you may believe, and what those women's rags claim, that isn't true. Along *with* sex, we want the same things women want. But because we tend to think with our penises, we can't always remember what those other things are.

Which was why I'd turned to these mags. But if they couldn't offer decent advice about relationships, where could I get the help I needed?

I hated to think that my romantic success depended on a costume czarina and a makeup goddess, neither of whom, to my knowledge, were in steady relationships, but who, Sam told me, were auditioning to write an online romantic advice column.

Be afraid, women of America, be very afraid.

On Sunday night, I headed back to the city. Traffic was bumper-to-bumper on the LIE, and during the all-too-frequent stops I memorized my lines for the new play, a meaty role that I could really sink my teeth into.

Then I checked my v-mail messages. My agent, who had some scripts for me to look at. Phoebe, who excitedly told me she was excited about working with me. Sheli, who let me know that she'd arrived in the city several days earlier than expected, and in an unexpected pique asked: where was I? It seemed everyone I knew in Manhattan had checked in. Except Megan. No word on how the gutting of my apartment was going.

Okay, so what would I say to Megan when I next saw her?

*"The apartment's really looking good."*

What I hoped she'd hear: You're looking good.

What she will hear: The apartment's really looking good.

*"I was thinking maybe double sinks in the bathroom."*

What I hoped she'd hear: Just in case I decide on a permanent roommate.

What she will hear: Figures. Another change in the plans.
*"I've got an extra ticket for opening night."*

What I hoped she'd hear: I miss you. I miss us together.
What she will hear: ?

It was that question mark that really bothered me.

Back in the city, I shoved Achilles into the elevator without the usual problems. Neither of us, it seemed, was in the mood to climb stairs.

Despite the fact that I couldn't keep my eyes open, I was anxious to see how much progress had been made on the renovation while I was away. Before I'd left, I'd dutifully selected new kitchen cabinets and wood flooring, shuffled through packs of paint chips and even picked out stainless steel appliances for my one new kitchen.

So imagine my surprise when I opened the front door and was greeted by this: a totally gutted and extremely large space where my apartment had once been. Except for a bedroom and the adjoining small bath, I could not find a solid wall, or stand on a floor that didn't feel as though I would go tumbling down into the apartment below.

Don't panic! I told myself. You're deep into a major renovation. You knew the apartment would be basically unlivable and you still chose to live here.

I found a note taped between the fireplace mantels.

Jack. Sheli stopped by. We had a nice chat.—M
P.S. I borrowed some newspaper that had your name boldfaced. For the bottom of the cat's litter box.

I wasn't going to panic. Yet.

# 7

*Megan*

SOME ADVICE TO keep in mind whenever you're feeling romantically challenged:

a) Indulge in power shopping. It provides immediate gratification.
b) Do not, under any circumstances, agree to be a bridesmaid.

Caveat:

Power shopping will never replace good sex with Mr. Right, Mr. Right Now or Mr. Maybe.

Trivia:

The number of bridesmaid dresses buried deep in one's closet is in direct proportion to the number of ex-boyfriends in one's life.

During WAM times (that's Without A Man) I've power shopped with $$ I've earned, $$$ I've saved, or $$$$ on the Available Credit line of my most recent credit card statement. Purchases acquired during any given shopathon were always in direct proportion to the volume of my romantic angst.

Which, these days, was at a lifetime high.

I'd spent the past few days analyzing and reanalyzing my latest conversation with Jack. You know, the one where he'd followed me into the subway and made an attempt at apologizing for his lack of empathy. I'm still wondering, if he'd gone as far as trailing me through Penn Station, would I have invited him out to Jersey for Sunday dinner with the Sullivans?

I don't know.

What I do know is, I wasn't kidding when I'd told Jack I wasn't going to shed tears for him anymore. Except I wasn't supposed to tell him I'd cried over him. I didn't have the strength to analyze the reasons *why*, since I was supposed to be channeling all my energy into Getting On With My Life.

But as I'd confided to Chloe, my friendship with Jack had been a big part of that life. I missed him, missed his friendship, his counsel, the way he made me laugh. The way he drove me crazy. Endlessly. And the way he understood me when no one else did or even tried.

Except everything changed between us because of S-E-X. And now I found myself attracted to him in a way that made a return to friendship unlikely—if not completely impossible. If I listened to my heart—and I was trying to do just that—it was telling me it hadn't healed from Jack's betrayal (the S-E-X).

So I'd decided to power shop.

On this Saturday morning, one of my power shopping partners was Sheli Bradshaw, Jack's new friend—as in *girl*—who was moving to the city, and was in town to check out apartments. According to several gossip rags, however, she's really waiting for Jack to invite her to live with him in the apartment that I'm designing and decorating for him. Not for Jack plus one.

But Jack had decamped to the Hamptons for the weekend. Sheli was alone. And I was either a brilliant strategist or a total idiot.

You be the judge.

Sometime between Sheli knocking on Jack's apartment door, demanding to know his whereabouts and telling me her life story in incoherent sound bites, she'd invited herself along on my shopping trip. That was after I managed to get in a few words, several of them mentioning that I was going to the Designer's Showcase at the Javits Convention Center to buy stuff for Jack's apartment.

Here's how our first meet began:

It was after seven on Friday night. I'd been staring at paint chips that ranged from calming greens to screaming reds, samples of maple flooring and granite countertops that might engage in friendly conversations with—rather than wage war on—green and/or red.

This is what single, professional women like me do when they are WAM. We color coordinate other people's lives.

Dinner had been a healthy portion of a large sausage and cheese pizza I'd shared with the construction crew, who'd reframed most of the interior walls of the apartment.

It had been a long but productive day, and I was ready to go home and chill out with a good book since I was dateless yet again. Friday nights can be…opportunities to catch up on personal projects. Or at least, that's what we unattached single women told ourselves.

But I was still at work, sitting cross-legged on the floor, finishing off another daily report that I'd leave for Jack to read when he got back from the Hamptons. Another daily report that, from all earlier indications, would remain unread. Men are so predictable.

The doorbell rang. Maybe the cute carpenter's apprentice, who'd spent most of the afternoon flirting with me while he plumbed the studs, had returned to help me finish off the pizza.

Don't get too excited. Plumbing the studs had nothing to do with sex and/or romance. It's construction-speak for checking that the wood framing was placed and nailed in straight. Although the carpenter-in-training was one stud who could have been plumbed, easily, if I'd been interested.

I opened the door.

"Excuse me," said a petite brunette dressed in a fashion style I can only describe as eye-opening California-lite-and-brite, "I'm looking for Jack Spencer."

"He's not here."

"That's okay. I'll wait." She pushed past me. The heady aroma of a trendy new perfume, which I'd nicknamed *I've No Shame, Take Me*, followed her.

Should I tell her about Jack's allergies to perfumes with cloying aromas—and women who were just plain cloying?

Yes. No.

Take a chance the info might wind up splattered on a billboard overlooking Times Square?

No. Yes.

"You might be waiting a while," I said matter-of-factly. "He's in the Hamptons this weekend."

Pout here. "Really? He forgot to tell me. I saw the lights, so I figured he was home."

"You're Sheli." I took a wild guess. "From L.A."

"Actually," she said with a Cheshire cat-like grin, "I'm a new New Yorker. Perhaps Jack mentioned that I'm a publicist with TopNotch Pictures? We've opened an East

Coast office. On Park and Fifty-third. I am so looking forward to meeting all of Jack's friends." (Significant pause.) "And you must be Megan, the decorator who's creating Jack's new home."

Her eyes grazed the room so quickly I wondered if she had a digital camera for a brain. "Doesn't look like you've made any progress."

You'll notice how it didn't get by me that she'd stuck me in a folder labeled "decorator," not "friend." And that, despite her nonchalance, Sheli knew my name. And I bet she'd memorized all the roles I'd played in the many chapters of Jack's life. Probably carried them in her Filofax under the heading "ex," as in, ex-friend, ex-lover, ex-everything.

"Progress is always difficult for the untrained eye to see. Notchtop Pictures?" (Mistake intentional.) "I've never heard of it. You guys do real movies?" (Easy smile offered here.) I could play the game, too. But I was tired, and not exactly at the top of my bitchy game.

*This overachieving dark-haired doll*, the slightly malicious little voice that had been spending a lot of time in my thoughts offered, *is the new woman Jack is dating. You tell him to leave you alone, and this is the best he can do? Can you imagine spending all those extended-family holiday dinners with her at the table? Or watching her bounce little Jacks on her knee after Jack has bounced all over her?*

And the answer to all of the above: no way.

But I'd given up all rights to interfere in Jack's life. Or had I?

If I listened to Vanessa, Jack was my downfall or my destiny.

If I listened to the two Ritas, I'd have walked down the aisle with Jack years ago, and they'd be happily showering my children with grandmotherly gifts, love and offers to babysit, so Jack and I could create more babies for them to spoil.

By spending time with Sheli, was I unconsciously searching for the one thing that made her irresistible to Jack? And then maybe I could replicate it? Or was I looking to reveal Sheli's fatal flaw—the one thing that I knew would drive Jack up a wall and out of the relationship?

Although I was an "ex" and Jack was my Big Mistake, I felt this unexplainable need to look out for his best interests. This didn't make sense, but then again, nothing about contemporary male-female relationships did. Which was one reason why we devour women's magazines.

Vanessa's phone message, *It can't be the same. But it can be better,* kept playing through my mind like a perky TV commercial jingle: once embedded in your memory, it wouldn't let go. I still didn't understand why *it* couldn't be the same, or better yet, why *it* couldn't go back to Before. Because Before was definitely better than Now. So, you see, I really did have a lot to think about.

But back to our power shopping trip.

The other shopper was Chloe, there to make sure I wouldn't:

a) buy anything Jack couldn't afford, or
b) do anything I might regret, including stuffing Sheli into a big, brown box marked "used goods" and shipping her, by slow freight, back to the West Coast.

Sheli, in my honest opinion, would not survive an actual New York minute. She came across as a pampered Valley Girl (no offense if you were one, or knew one, or aspired to be one), someone who needed the assistance of a strong male to guide her up and down Fifth Avenue. Provided she could find Fifth Avenue. (Hint: Traffic runs one way, downtown, dividing the east and west sides of Manhattan.)

Her idea of power shopping, as I understood it from her nonstop monologue, was cruising Rodeo Drive or the soundstages of Hollywood trailed by the unlucky personal assistant who got to carry her packages.

I was curious to see how she'd do in the take-no-prisoners atmosphere at the Designer's Showcase. Just imagine thousands of women loose in a major department store the day after Thanksgiving—and then double that number and the amount of money they're playing with.

During the cab ride to the convention center, Sheli told us exactly what Jack wanted and needed in his new apartment. "I've made a list, keeping it extremely minimalist, because Jack's personality is so forceful, he doesn't need lots of things."

"We do have a two-thousand-square-foot apartment to fill," I said diplomatically (a trait interior designers developed quickly or they tended to go out of business).

"But we'll fill it *minimally*." She leaned over to speak to the cab driver as we inched our way down Eleventh Avenue. "New York City is so congested. How do you people ever get anywhere? What you need is more freeways."

The look I exchanged with Chloe shouted, *On what planet did he find her?*

Chloe raised an eyebrow that told me, *Planet Hollyweird. Where else?*

Me (another pointed look), *Jack would never forgive me if I didn't make an attempt to save him.*

Chloe (with a nod), *Go for it!* Out loud, she said, "This should be a fun outing. Girls Shopping Smartly. If we don't finish today, we can always come back tomorrow."

Me, heavy sigh and a look that said, *No way!*

The cab finally pulled into the circular driveway in front of the Javits Center. Chloe paid the driver eleven bucks plus a very generous tip to reward him for *not* dropping us into the Hudson. ("The least I can do for you," she whispered in my ear.)

Sheli looked around frantically as we entered the cavernous convention hall packed with local designers. "Where's our personal shopper?"

I prodded her through the turnstile and waved my professional pass at the guard. "We're our own personal shoppers. That's what interior designers do. We shop so the client doesn't have to."

We spent the first hour searching for the perfect sofa for Jack's living room, among thousands of different styles, fabrics and colors. To the untrained, this can be overwhelming. And lead to appalling choices.

"I'm leaning toward a soft, dark leather," I said to Chloe. "A bit of contrast to the pear-green walls."

She relaxed into a chocolate-brown leather sofa. "Comfy. I like it."

"This one's perfect." Sheli grabbed my arm and pulled me across the aisle. "Black vinyl and chrome. So Jack. Don't you think so, Megan?"

I pretended not to hear.

Which led Sheli to then rave about the chrome tables covered with cracked glass, a black vinyl chair that morphed into a chaise lounge and several lamps that looked like rejects from a welding class on track lighting. If this was the way people really nested in L.A., intelligent life in that city was in big trouble.

After subjecting ourselves to thirty minutes of Sheli's lack of style, Chloe and I deposited her at the makeshift café, ordered her a double espresso and suggested she write down all of her suggestions.

Chloe and I returned to serious power shopping.

We next saw Sheli an hour later during our return trip to the café. She was busy talking on her cell phone. And her list now filled an entire sheet of letter-size paper.

"There can't be that much black vinyl in the universe," I said under my breath to Chloe.

"Alas," she said sadly, "there is."

I tapped Sheli on the shoulder. "We found a couple of lamps you might like."

"I can't stay." She urged me into the chair next to her. "This shopping experience has been wonderful, but there was a last-minute cancellation at The Spa, and I got an appointment thirty minutes from now for a facial and massage." Her voice dropped to a whisper. "You understand. I need to look my best for Jack."

I could only nod. Chloe looked like she was going to burst out laughing.

"Take my list." Sheli waved the paper at me, then she lowered her voice to a whisper. "And do your designing magic."

I nodded again. Stuffed her shopping list in my tote.

We silently walked Sheli to the escalator and made sure she caught a taxi. ("The Spa," I told him. "Fifth Avenue and Fifty-seventh." Although I was mighty tempted to say, "Lincoln Tunnel, and don't stop until you hit the Pacific Ocean.") Chloe and I watched as the cab disappeared into the mess of traffic going uptown on Eleventh Avenue. I doubted Sheli would make it to her facial on time. Not my problem.

"You ready to really shop?" Chloe asked.

We made a quick circle around the display areas, placed the order for Jack's furniture and then caught the Thirty-fourth Street bus to Macy's. Because after my short time with Sheli, I needed a personal power shopping fix—cost no object. I'd worry later about the continued health of my credit card.

Chloe steered me toward the cosmetic, fine jewelry and leather goods counters. I purchased bubble bath, bath oils and bath salts, several aromatherapy candles, a pair of eighteen-carat gold and pearl earrings, a matching bracelet and a red leather clutch purse (designer of the moment).

We then decamped to our favorite diner just around the corner on Eighth Avenue.

"Feel better?" Chloe asked.

I slipped into the booth. "Yes. It's been quite a day."

Before the waitress could hand me a menu I placed my order. "Double order macaroni and cheese. Large chocolate phosphate."

Chloe rolled her eyes. "You're so bad. No mac and cheese, too many carbs. No chocolate death. Make that two Greek salads. Two large iced teas. Heavy on the ice."

I sipped the ice water the waitress had left. "We power shop when we're in romantic angst. What do you think men do?"

"They fortify their manliness by buying a huge power tool, driving a snazzy sports car or seeing how many women they can score with," Chloe said. "Sometimes they do all three."

"I've been wondering… Do you think Jack felt about Trey the way I feel about Sheli?"

"How's that?"

"She's so unworthy of him. Brittle. Humorless. So not the kind of girl I thought Jack would end up with."

"He won't. End up with her. Because she's a segue."

"An interesting term. Segue. You know this because…?"

"You'll see for yourself once we play a little game called Our Shopping Trip."

I whimpered. "Please. Anything but that."

"Just the high points," Chloe said. "I promise you won't be disappointed. Hand over Sheli's list."

I slid the paper across the table.

Chloe read. "Sleeper sofa in black vinyl, chrome frame. Glass coffee table, glass end tables. More chrome. Lots of track lighting. Ceramic tile floors." She shuddered. "Feels like I'm shopping from a Bad Movie Scenery catalogue. Your turn."

I pulled out our list from my tote. "Camelback leather sofa, rich chocolate-brown. A matching macho chair and ottoman in deep red. Two cool floor lamps, and end tables, all a little eclectic but keeping with the mission style of the room."

Champion power shopping, if I have to say so myself. I'd made a huge dent in my romantic malaise and created a nice hole in Jack's bank account, as well.

"Sheli's selections are a mishmash of minimalism. Ours, mission-style elegance. What does this tell you?"

I shrugged.

"C'mon, Megan, this is a slam dunk."

I compared the two lists. And a light bulb went off. "She's shopping for Logan Hunter."

"This is his apartment on *The D.A. Chronicles*, down to the awful track lighting. You don't have to see it to know the man has a king-size water bed."

"So that means I'm shopping for Jack Spencer. Who hates track lighting. Gets seasick on water beds. She's shopping for a narcissistic character in a TV drama."

"Now, what have you learned from our little game?"

"Sheli has no clue as to who Jack is."

"And," Chloe prompted.

"She's a segue."

"Good. And what else?"

"The next time she wants to play girlfriends, I'll dump her onto the Number Seven subway train, and send her off to the mini-mall in Flushing. Shipping her back to the West Coast wouldn't be as entertaining."

"Exactly what I'd do. You're my kind of girl."

The waitress delivered our iced teas. I reached for Sheli's shopping list and placed it directly in the center of the table. Then dropped my glass on it. Chloe and I watched as the condensation dripped onto the paper and smudged all the ink. Goodbye to Sheli's list.

"You think she'll tell Jack about today?" Chloe asked.

"Only if she wants him to know she can't keep up with us."

Chloe raised her glass in a toast. "Those West Coast girls have no city grit."

"True. I wonder what Jack sees in her."

"Tits," Chloe said knowingly.

First-class tits. "I wonder how much she paid for them."

"You can ask."

"You think she'll tell?"

"Depends. On how much she wants to impress you, and how much she's already impressed Jack." Pause. "You owe me big-time."

That I did. I held up my overflowing shopping bag. "You helped me find good stuff to fill the holes in my lonely life."

Chloe rolled her eyes. "That's not what I meant, and you know it. Trust me, there are not enough baths left in your lifetime to use up that stuff. If you need another shopping fix, I suggest the Meat-Packing District. On a Friday or Saturday night."

CHLOE'S SUGGESTION KEPT coming back to me for days after the shopping trip.

Since the night of our women's group, she had been hinting, strongly, that I should let Jack ease back into my life as though he'd never been gone, and let him think it was *his* idea.

And if I wasn't up to that, find someone new.

She's primed for helping me manipulate Jack for the former, or power shop for the latter.

The latter being The Perfect Man Who's Not Jack But Makes My Heart Go Zing.

Wanna bet either choice is going to cost a lot more than I can afford, financially and emotionally?

But what did I have to lose?

I had very little experience with blind dates, and for good reason. I didn't do 'em. That went for fix-ups with other people's brothers/cousins/friends and you-name-him. Now I should add clients to that list. That's how I met my ex-fiancé, when the design firm I used to work for sent me over to his Wall Street company to refurbish their offices.

If you stretch the term "blind date," he was one, and we all know that did not end in happily ever after.

It's been more than six months since I've had a date—blind or otherwise. I'm not complaining. Just stating the facts. I didn't consider my night of sex with Jack a date. More like an interlude. But not a segue. We had too much history for me to be merely a segue.

Speaking of Jack, I haven't heard from him, or seen him, since he got back from the Hamptons. It's been more than a week. I guess when he's not rehearsing for his new play, he's busy dating Sheli and showing her the real New York.

(See any gossip tab in NYC, all currently running Jack Spencerathons.)

Me? Since my power shopping trip last weekend, I've spent my free time regretting I'd ever agreed to be a bridesmaid. (See b above.) And I'd been putting off picking up The Dress That I Will Never Wear Again until the last minute. The last minute being tonight, mere hours before the rehearsal dinner.

Ah, yes, welcome to another dateless Friday night. If you're counting, and I was, that made—let's see, from the Friday after New Year's Eve to late June—twenty in a row.

I could see the relief on the wedding consultant's face when Chloe and I entered the dress shop less than an hour before closing. She had the gown ready. And the ridiculously expensive shoes that had been dyed to match. All I needed to do was try both on to make sure the hem hit "just so," just so I wouldn't trip down the aisle.

Chloe and I followed her into the back of the shop, where there was a large dressing area with dozens of mirrors. With the help of a sales associate, I shrugged out of my clothes and into a sleeveless satin dress that, with my red hair, had me looking like a piece of day-old cotton candy from Coney Island.

"That's an interesting pink," Chloe said.

"The alternatives were a bright tangerine that made us all wince, and an off-lime that reminded me of algae," I said as the sales associate nipped and tucked. "I'm only doing this because she caught me at a weak moment."

"Who's getting married?"

"The bride-to-be is one of my wedding guests-who-wasn't."

"The one who offered to throw your unwedding reception?"

"You got it. Right after she fired her wedding planner."

I'll forgo all modesty here. I had started a new NYC trend: take back your wedding, or risk losing your husband-to-be. Following a brief mention early last February in the *Times* Sunday Styles section (complete with a pithy quote), several brides-to-be called to let me know they'd done just that. A few followed up with design inquiries that could translate into new business.

"Whatever did you do with all the bridesmaid dresses? You know, that was classy, buying them all back."

"Don't tell Mrs. Flannery, but I retrofitted the dresses so they're now her new bedroom curtains, king-size duvet cover and bed skirt."

"Like I said, classy." Chloe motioned me to twirl, so I twirled.

"Do you think I look like a slightly used candy cane, or inedible cotton candy?" I asked.

"Yes to both," Chloe said. "When's the wedding?"

"What are you doing tomorrow night?"

"Washing my hair? Renting a movie?"

That was code for WAM.

"Come with me to the wedding." I motioned her to unzip the dress, which slithered to the floor, much to the dismay of the wedding consultant. I slipped back into my jeans and tee and followed her out to the front of the store. While the consultant and her assistant carefully packed the dress and shoes, I whipped out my credit card to pay for them.

"What's on the menu?"

We both knew she didn't mean food.

"Tonight's the first time I'm seeing most of these people since…you know when." Pause. "I'll be okay alone at the rehearsal dinner. But I could use some moral support at the wedding reception."

"Jack going to be there?" Chloe reached for the shoes.

I shouldered the bulky vinyl dress bag. "You are so wise."

"Let me guess. He's in the wedding party."

"No, but he's invited. And he accepted, for two." The bride-to-be, an old high school friend, figured since I was WAM I'd rather hang out with Jack than with a perfect stranger. But then she'd read last week that Jack was involved with another woman, so she'd invited me to bring a date.

"I'm there for you." Chloe squeezed my shoulder. "Just tell me the time and place."

The rehearsal dinner went well. Connected with old friends who, bless them all, never mentioned Trey. Or Jack. Sipped diet soda during the endless toasts. Hit up several times...for my business card. And managed to stay out of the way of a former star football player whose nickname had been Octopus, and for whom nothing had changed. On the way home, alone, I vowed it would be my last time as a member of someone else's wedding party until I got my turn.

The wedding ceremony itself, which was held at a small nondenominational church on Madison Avenue, took all of ten minutes. On to the reception...

It was held at the Plaza Hotel, a place I hadn't visited in more than six months. Trey had proposed there. We'd planned to have our wedding reception in the Grand Ballroom.

I sucked in a deep breath and straightened my shoulders as Chloe and I walked inside the hotel. We greeted the concierge with the matinee-idol looks, whom I recognized as last week's murder victim on *The D.A. Chronicles*. And who, if he remembered me as a bride dumped right before her wedding day, didn't let on.

We marched up the stairs and headed to the ballroom.

My radar bypassed the bride and locked right onto Jack. Who was, of course, with Sheli.

I'd been so busy being a bridesmaid, I hadn't seen them during the ceremony, so this was my first chance to check out how they looked together. (I wasn't counting the photos of them in celeb magazines that will remain unnamed.)

Jack's hair was a little mussed, but other than that, he looked as though he'd just stepped out of a *GQ* photo shoot. His charcoal-gray suit jacket molded to his broad shoulders, and the rest of him didn't look too bad either.

Sheli wore a sleeveless sapphire dress that looked as though it had been painted on. It showed every curve, natural and enhanced, and then some.

I searched for something about the two of them that didn't work. Finally settled on, "I hate that they sorta look like Barbie and Ken."

Was it a coincidence that all the women I'd seen Jack with since we'd had sex had been the same—size zeros in brunette or blond? Did Jack have something against dating redheads? Or was it just me?

"She's so wrong for him," I said.

"Jack will figure that out," Chloe said. "But it's a toss-up whether it'll be before or after they have sex."

Then Jack smiled at something Sheli said. I couldn't see his dimples but I knew they were there. It was the smile he bestowed whenever he genuinely liked the person he was with.

I felt my heart drop. Then it bumped and thumped. I got goose bumps, the kind that you get when you're both nervous and excited. And then I felt this little sizzle of electricity, which seemed to bounce off me, across the room, and hit Jack squarely in the back.

It must have really happened, because he suddenly turned away from Sheli and stared straight at me. But he didn't smile.

Sheli's eagle eyes followed. And she possessively wrapped her arm through his.

"She's not sleeping with him," Chloe said under her breath. "But not for her lack of trying."

"How can you tell?" I couldn't keep my eyes off them. Especially once Jack's arm, now casually wrapped around Sheli's shoulders, drew her closer to him.

"She's hanging much too hard," Chloe explained. "She's insecure about the relationship. Knows you two have a backstory that's complicated. She doesn't know for sure if you've slept together, but she thinks you have. So she keeps touching him to be sure he's still there with her. And not here with you."

"She doesn't have to worry. Jack doesn't like me much now."

"Megan, walk over there and ask Jack to dance."

"There's no music."

"Who cares?"

"Jack doesn't like to dance." Which had always surprised me, because he loved to perform. "Besides, he's got his arms around another woman, and it's a sure bet they'll be locking lips before too long."

"Your point?"

"He's going to see it as a ploy to talk with him."

"Yes." She nudged me. "Go over there. Now. Before he decides she'd make a good bed partner tonight."

I couldn't do it.

Seeing Jack with Sheli, the two looking like they'd just stepped off the top of a wedding cake, just knocked all the stuffing out of me. Before the night of our Big Mistake, I'd have felt obligated to share my feelings about any woman Jack had brought into his life. I'd have felt comfortable going up to them and joining the conversation, being Jack's best friend.

I'd never hesitated before, so what stopped me now?

It was the painful chill that ran through me as Jack swept Sheli into his arms and they moved in sync onto the dance floor.

Even before the music started.

# 8

*Jack*

WHAT FOLLOWS IS AN EXAMPLE of art imitating (or parodying) life. My life.

Him (sprawled in front of balance beam): Won't you say 'I'm sorry'?

Her (with a bright smile): I'm sorry you didn't fall harder on your ass.

Him (picking himself up): Go ahead, mock me! But I want this, want us, to work.

Her (raising beam higher): Only in your dreams.

*Knock at door. Enter second Her.*

Second Her (hands Him a long piece of paper): There. Our life together. All plotted out. Just sign on the dotted line and I'll take care of everything.

Him (abruptly to second Her): Not now. (Pleading to Her): What about our history?

*Knock at door. Enter second Him.*

Second Him (to Her): Aha! I'm not the only one sending you conflicting messages.

Her (walking unsteadily but successfully across beam): Not to worry. I'm no longer listening to either of you.

*Second Him exits.*

Him (trying to be tough and pleading at same time): C'mon, I'm just a guy. Gimme a break.

Her and second Her roll their eyes. And exit.

Him (attempting to get on beam, falling off. Again. And again.): Am I that out of touch?

*Curtain.*

If you think this sounded familiar, you're not the only one. It's the final page of Act I of *Out of Touch*, the new (and rather dark) comedy I was currently rehearsing.

When I wasn't stumbling through the art-imitating-life dialogue, I was writing (and rewriting) opening-night review blurbs in my head:

"Who's the perfect romantic hero? Jack Spencer."
—*New York Times*

"Jack Spencer shows just how in touch he is with his feelings in *Out of Touch*."
—*Variety*

All part of the art of pretending.

When our director cut us loose for the union-mandated sixty-minute lunch, everyone else scattered. I leaned over the edge of the stage and peered into the half-lit theater.

"So, what ya think?" I asked Sam Davies, who'd stopped by to watch me go through my paces.

"You might want to ask the playwright what technique he used to record the sorry state of your love life."

See. I wasn't the only one who'd noticed.

I hopped down off the stage and joined Sam in a slouch in the front row. "Is every straight guy out there as clueless as me?"

"Rhetorical question?"

"You bet." Pause. "But I have to wonder if the playwright is one of Sheli's stable of exes."

Sam choked back a chuckle. "Well, I know I'm basing this on a quick first impression... But she does display signs of a woman out to dominate the world. Especially the world of men."

"Definitely not the woman of my dreams." I thought a moment. "More like the woman of my nightmares."

Sam nodded in understanding.

I suppose you want to know what happened at the wedding.

Sheli came with me. Not that I wouldn't have invited her anyway, but she'd picked up the invitation I'd tossed onto one of the fireplace mantels and, as she flashed it in front of my face, told me she'd love to meet some of my friends.

Made sense to me. It was time to see how she fit into the rest of my life, keeping in mind how Sheli had underwhelmed my parents. In particular, my mother, who'd confided not long ago that her offer to give Sheli the secret potato salad recipe had been a test—one Sheli had failed miserably.

Megan's cryptic note, "Sheli stopped by. We had a nice chat," had left plenty of room for interpretation, too. Although I didn't know it at the time, Megan had formed some strong negative opinions about Sheli. (I want to thank Chloe Farrell for finally setting me straight on what really happened during the infamous power shopping trip.)

But first, the wedding. Sheli and I sat in the back of the church and watched as Megan did her thing as a bridesmaid. Only someone who knew her as well as I did could understand how difficult it was for her to play the role. Trey's betrayal had sucked something vital out of her. And, because of what happened between Megan and me last New Year's Eve, it appeared as though I'd been chosen to stand in permanently as the major villain in her personal drama. Not a part I enjoyed playing.

I wanted to talk to her. Clear the air once and for all. Had picked up the phone dozens of times to call, even punched out her number. But truthfully, I didn't think we could have a conversation that didn't end in us arguing.

But maybe we could converse nicely among our mutual friends during the wedding reception. Except, whenever there was the possibility for a connection, Sheli managed to drag me off in the opposite direction, including onto the dance floor (I hate to dance!) before the music started playing.

Looking back, I must have been the only person at the wedding reception who didn't see then that Sheli considered Megan a threat. (Thanks again to Chloe for pointing that out.) So I allowed myself to casually cruise through the next couple of weeks with Sheli. That is, until my eyes were finally opened to the realities of a relationship with her.

My nightmare took form the evening of an industry-only movie screening for a new film from TopNotch Pictures. Invitation-only screening followed by invitation-only party. I was able to score another invite, and gave it to Sam.

Sam had skipped the movie, but showed up at the after-party at Cooler, one of the hip clubs in the Meat-Packing District. So he'd witnessed (and been subjected to) the somewhat dark side of Sheli that worried me.

Several of her former West Coast colleagues were at the party, and from the body language exchanged, I could tell she'd traded a lot more than "good mornings" with all of them, and would be happy to do so again beginning that night.

So much for her claims of wanting "a fulfilling monogamous relationship."

Unless, of course, I was ready and willing to slip between the sheets with her. Which I wasn't. I'd sorta figured out that my having sex with a woman meant different things to different women. So I was being extra cautious here.

I was worried Sheli might see any kind of intimacy beyond kissing as an engraved invitation to pick out a china pattern.

(She was already imagining his/her sinks in the master bath, suggesting wallpaper patterns and talking about the added value of having—and letting someone else raise—her two-point-five kids in the same breath as she discussed climbing her way up the movie studio's food chain. All of which, in case you don't get to see my play, was on the "list" the second Her handed me at the end of Act I.)

Back to Sheli's dark side. Right in the middle of my conversation with a major gossip columnist, who, with a word or two in print could make or break my career, Sheli pulled me onto the dance floor (against my will, same as she did at the wedding reception). She then loudly bitched about the woman who'd been promoted into her former job. The gossip columnist salivated in delight.

Other samples:

"I've got a brilliant idea," Sheli gleefully said when we got back to the table where all her exes sat. "I know (name of nationally influential movie critic here) is going to hate the movie. So let's keep him from seeing it until after his deadline. No opening-day review!"

Her colleagues raised their glasses in toast.

She then turned to Sam, to whom she'd been introduced not more than fifteen minutes ago. "Do I know you?" Pause. "Oh. You're one of those New York TV actors, aren't you?"

"One of those TV actors," I put in mildly, "who's just been signed to co-star in TopNotch's movie filming here this fall."

"Oh. Silly me." She fawned all over Sam. "So many people to meet, so little time." Heavy sigh. "We must do lunch."

"Have your personal assistant get in touch with mine," Sam drawled in a honeyed tone of voice, one that told me he wasn't fooled at all.

What had impressed me about Sheli back in February— her quick wit, her stylish looks and her fascination with me—all seemed cold and calculated now.

And that's exactly what I said to Sam.

Who said, of course, "I told you so. Think about it. She's your Trey."

Trey, of course, being Megan's fiancé-who-dumped-her. The guy whose popularity quotient with friends and immediate family topped out at zero.

Sheli wasn't faring any better, with my family or my friends. Or for that matter, Manhattan's gossip columnists. (See all of last week's Page Six, and the weekly tabs, including a cover blurb in the *Star*. )

My conclusion: Sheli Bradshaw was no Megan Sullivan. After several restless nights, I'd decided no matter how hard I imagined it, I couldn't see spending the next fifty years with Sheli. Or living the next fifty years without Megan in my life.

So all I needed now was a plan. One guaranteed to work. Which was part of the reason Sam had come by today.

"Ready for lunch?" Sam asked.

"Lunch, yes. Alicia and Rachel as my new image consultants, not really." Pause. "How much have you told them?"

"Just enough."

"Just enough of what?"

"A detail here. A detail there. Enough so they understand you messed up big-time with Megan. And you're desperate. You got everything you need?"

I patted the envelope in my back pocket.

"Relax," Sam advised. "This is going to be painless."

"And good for you," I muttered. Platitudes the two Ritas dished out whenever they knew Megan and I weren't going to buy whatever they were selling. "Tell me again why I've agreed to this."

"Because you messed up big-time with Megan and have no clue how to fix it."

Good point.

We were meeting Alicia and Rachel at a tiny Hell's Kitchen burgers-only restaurant frequented by theater types. I'd (strongly) vetoed meeting at the Times Square Spencer's because I didn't want anyone I knew, or who knew my family, to find out I was listening to advice from a pair of amateur counselors.

Amateur counselors, I have to add, who looked like characters out of *The Rocky Horror Picture Show.*

The tall and lanky Rachel was dressed head to toe in tight black leather. Her dark brown hair was highlighted with huge chunks of blond, with a mishmash of metallic colors thrown in for, I guessed, effect.

Alicia had a shocking-pink sweatband around her forehead that clashed with her shocking-red hair, which I thought had been blond the last time I saw her. Maybe not. This color had to be a joke gift from a bottle, because Mother Nature couldn't be that cruel. She wore a long, tie-dyed T-shirt over plaid denim pants. Whatever fashion statement she was after did not compute with me.

By contrast, Sam, dressed in red-and-blue denim biker gear and with his blond hair in spikes, looked positively normal.

"Where do we begin?" I asked brightly once we'd decided between rare, medium or well-done burgers.

"Define your style," Alicia ordered.

"He has no style," sniffed Rachel.

She should talk. Would you put yourself in the hands of a woman who wore all black leather in the heat of summer? Look, I was in the middle of rehearsals, and no one expected me to be a *fashionista* (see current issue of any women's magazine for further explanation) until I was in front of a paying audience. And I liked my faded jeans, stretched-out T-shirt (my lucky Bad Boys one) and beat-up Nikes.

My hair was one color—dark brown—and that color was natural. And naturally mine.

No one else sitting at the table could claim the same.

"Maybe we should start with your qualifications," I said to Rachel, who appeared to be the leader of this pack.

"We're women," Rachel said. "We know what women want."

"Either of you in a successful romantic relationship?" Sam asked before I could.

The two women looked at each other. Then back at us guys as though we were life-forms from another planet. Which perhaps, from their perspective, we were.

"We're in something better," Alicia said with a touch of smugness. "We're online Web goddesses for the romantically challenged."

"In particular, the romantically challenged male." Rachel looked deep into my eyes. "Which you, Jack, definitely are."

"But we're willing to work with you," Alicia chimed in.

"Because you do have potential," Rachel said graciously.

"And a rising 'Q Factor,'" Alicia pointed out.

"Once we fix you, the rest of your gender will be a piece of cake." Rachel toasted me with her glass of water.

"They're kidding, right?" I turned to Sam.

Alicia pulled out a copy of *Chic* that had all these little colored tabs sticking out from its pages. She slid the mag across the table.

I opened the magazine to the first tabbed page, which was an article on dating. "Signs to Guide You Through Guy-land."

Rachel slapped at my hand. "I'll summarize. Women equate finding the perfect man to buying a pair of knock-out, kick-your-ass shoes. They want stylish, a little dangerous to walk in, but in the end, comfort is everything."

"Trying on pairs of shoes is like dating," Alicia said. "Some don't quite fit even though you want 'em badly. Some fit but don't look right."

"What looks like a bargain is anything but," Rachel said. "Wear 'em once, wear 'em twice, maybe, and then you might have to toss 'em."

"Although, sometimes you might give the pair that's wrong for you to your best friend," Alicia put in.

Rachel looked horrified. "You wouldn't." Pause. "Have you?"

"Sure. Just the other week. She is so in love. And I feel so good about the match."

While the two of them were discussing the merits of giving things away, I turned to Sam. "Are we talking about buying shoes here, or women dating men? And how does fixing my relationship with Megan fit in?"

"Shoes, no. Dating, I don't know."

Rachel rapped on the table. "Pay attention. Our women's mantra is to never settle for less than perfect. But what's perfect for me isn't necessarily perfect for Alicia. I've been trying on all types of shoes—all by myself—since I was fourteen, and have yet to find that ideal pair."

"Why am I not surprised?" Sam muttered under his breath.

"So if you equate buying shoes with dating, you take it to the next level," Alicia said. "Try on as many as you can, as fast as you can. Which means speed dating."

"Was dating this confusing in the twentieth century?" I asked, a bit disingenuously.

Alicia offered a pitiful look. "It's not complicated if you know The Code. You speed date. After you find the one you think is the one, you use The Code. In your case, use The Code with Megan."

I leaned back, gazing at the two women. "You'll give it up?"

"For a price," Rachel said smugly.

Of course. I slid the envelope across the table.

Alicia waved it in front of Rachel.

Who grabbed it. "This had better be two tickets each, front row center, to opening night of your off-Broadway play. Plus invites to the cast party."

Once the tickets and invites had been examined, we were back to the subject at hand, fixing me.

"Jack, you do have real clothes, right?" Alicia sounded very worried. To Rachel, "Can we borrow his wardrobe from the show?" Back to me, "Because this is a three-step program. How you *look*. What you *say*. What you *do*."

"Then, presto!" Rachel waved her hands in imitation of a magic wand. "From heterosexual into metrosexual."

It's so very New York to be a met-sex these days. A met-sex, you see, is a straight guy open to new ideas about himself. Rumor has it he's on the search for his inner being, borrowing the best from the gay aesthetic (that fashion and taking care of your body is not just girl stuff anymore).

Still, my confusion must have shown. "Whatever happened to guys just being guys?"

"Pretend," Sam suggested.

"It's gonna be okay," Rachel counseled me in a soothing voice. "You've got us now."

Not exactly a confidence builder, but they were all I had.

Alicia pulled a spiral notebook out of her bag and ripped out a piece of paper. "The next time you're alone with Megan, do everything on this list, in exactly this order. No deviations."

"What is this?" I asked.

"It's The Code," Rachel explained.

"Memorize it," Alicia said. "Then burn it."

"Sorta like *Mission: Impossible*," Sam muttered.

Without reading The Code, I folded the paper in half and tucked it in my wallet.

The check paid (my treat), we left. Rachel and Alicia headed for the subway. Sam followed me as I ducked over to the newsstand and grabbed copies of the latest chick mags.

Sam looked over my shoulder and read one of the covers. "Ninety-Nine Man Clues. Sure signs he'll be a good lover, a good husband, or maybe good for nothing." Pause. "Sure you need this?"

"Insurance," I said dryly. I handed over a twenty to the newsstand guy and had change trickled into my palm in return.

"Ye of little faith." Sam shook his head in dismay.

"Here's hoping I'll live through this experiment without regretting it."

Sam leaned back and studied me with the intensity of a real detective. "What is gain without pain?"

A question I debated later that evening as I surveyed my personal money pit.

There's a movie by that title. A comedy, actually (although I didn't do much laughing while watching it), about a New York City couple forced out of their apartment, who then naively buy a fixer-upper in the suburbs and watch as all hell breaks loose.

After I got home from the theater, I settled myself in the bedroom I'd been using. I stuck the video in the combo DVD-VHS player, and for the next ninety minutes Achilles and I noshed on popcorn and diet cola and watched what could be my life (starring a much younger Tom Hanks) play out in front of me, on a thirty-two-inch plasma TV screen.

Sheer torture. Not the movie itself, but the process of watching two hapless New Yorkers trying to turn a dilapidated house into a home.

"Why would anyone in their right mind renovate?" I asked Achilles as the credits rolled across the screen. "And then try to mix building a relationship with rebuilding a house?"

In response, the dog brought me his leash for our final walk of the evening. As I started to shut the door, I gazed back into the mess inside. So much left to do. So much money spent. So little time, if we were going to make our deadline (end of the twenty-first century).

We were well into July and I was living (barely) through renovation hell, and slowly losing my mind.

I'M NOT AT MY BEST WHEN I haven't gotten enough sleep. Assume cranky. So when I heard noises coming from the living room before eight o'clock on a weekend morning, I wasn't thinking, "Oh, good, company."

One door slammed. Then another. Followed by the

sound of something heavy being dragged across the newly sanded hardwood floors.

Achilles stuck his nose through the partly opened bedroom door, wagged his tail, then padded back to his doggy bed by the window and closed his eyes. So much for my guard dog.

I tossed off the comforter and rummaged through the pile of stuff on the floor until I came up with my cell phone. I was just about to punch out 9-1-1 when my bedroom door burst open and in walked two workers carrying a maple kitchen cabinet.

Which looked exactly like the cabinets Megan had ordered after we'd argued endlessly about what would look best in the kitchen. Natural or faux finish? Dark wood or light? Finally, I'd closed my eyes, stuck my finger in a catalog and pointed. The fact that these cabinets were maple, and not the knotty pine I'd picked, was testament to Megan's good taste and patience.

Back to the cabinet carriers.

Toss-up as to which of the three of us (four, if you count Achilles) was more surprised. After all, I wasn't dressed for visitors. There I was, sitting on the edge of my bed, wearing my boxer shorts with the red hearts, and the aqua Bad Boy T-shirt I was so fond of.

After a long pause, the taller one said in a squeaky female voice, "So not the kitchen."

The other worker, also a woman, took one look at me and giggled. As the two of them eased back out the doorway, I heard one of them say, "He's a lot sexier on TV than he is in person."

These days everyone is a critic.

I grabbed a towel (from the freshly laundered pile that threatened to fall off the chair that was slowly losing its stuffing) and wrapped it around my waist. Cautiously, I got out of bed. I peered around the door and saw a path of cabinets on the floor that started at the front door and led to what would soon be my new kitchen.

The piercing sound of a drill drove me back to my bedroom. I grabbed the cell and punched out Megan's number. If she didn't answer (or if a man answered) I didn't know what I'd do.

"Whoever you are, this had better be an emergency," she snarled into my ear. There was a rustle of bedcovers. And a thump that sounded like she'd fallen out of bed.

"It's Jack."

"Like I said, an emergency."

"Hello to you, too. Thought you'd like to know that strangers are installing cabinets in my kitchen."

"I'm sure I told you they were coming this morning."

No, she hadn't. This didn't seem like a good time to remind her she hadn't been in touch. At all.

Anyway, she hung up. I was about to hit the redial button when the phone rang.

"I'm trying to reach Jack Spencer," said the unfamiliar female voice on the other end of the line. "Are you him?"

"Depends. Who's this?"

She rattled off her name and the phrase *Biography* TV show. Don't ask me why I'd agreed to be a *Biography* subject, but both Ritas thought it meant I'd "arrived in show biz," and the story of my life would, naturally, include several mentions of them.

Sam had also agreed to talk about me, and the show's producer was just confirming that the crew would meet them—not me, I wasn't invited—at the Sullivan home in Montclair the second Sunday in August for a first round of interviews. The location had been Rita 1's suggestion, which the producer thought would work well as a backdrop.

Rita 1 then promptly called, excited about the upcoming interviews, and invited me to Montclair for dinner. She didn't mention if Megan would be there. Or not.

My parents would be interviewed at their condo in Florida.

And Megan? She'd been contacted, but so far hadn't agreed to speak on my behalf. I was confident, however, that she would. If only for the chance to get her feelings about me out in front of millions of strangers.

Most of the details sealed, I was ready to face the workers who'd taken over my apartment.

As I've mentioned before, actors have to develop a lack of inhibitions. So while the crew—which now included several carpenters creating bookshelves for my study— continued to put my house back together, I showered, put on a pair of disreputable-looking jeans from the clean laundry pile and shuffled Achilles out of the apartment for a walk and a huge breakfast.

This morning I did takeout from Spencer's. Then Achilles and I headed over to Riverside Park. After every squirrel on the Upper West Side had played hide-and-seek with Achilles, we trekked back to the apartment.

Two hours away hadn't improved the home scene.

I had thought the inside of my Upper West Side oasis was a disaster, but the outside didn't look any better, with trucks competing for the limited street parking, and work crews (electricians, plumbers, carpenters of all shapes and sizes) hangin' around, waiting for their turn to siphon off large amounts of my disposable income.

My neighbors had had the good sense to decamp for their summer homes in the Hamptons or the country.

Leaving me with my personal Money Pit.

I wondered if the filmmakers would consider a sequel. And if my savvy agent could negotiate me a screenwriting credit as well as a starring role. It wouldn't take much pretending on my part to convince them I'd be perfect as the overstressed homeowner who wished he'd never started this project.

But then, I wouldn't be where I was with Megan.

Which, I reminded myself, wasn't anywhere at all.

Achilles dragged me the final few yards to my front stoop, where—surprise!—Megan, dressed in an outfit that resembled painter's overalls, sat with her head in her hands. I recognized the curly red hair, which was covered by a paint-splattered baseball cap (New York Yankees) that once belonged to me.

It was only when Achilles tried to plant himself on her lap that she looked up. Wanly.

"Oh. You're back." Pause. "I'm sorry I haven't been in touch about the renovation."

Her way of communicating over the past few weeks had been to leave me detailed daily progress reports, which made about as much sense to me as floor plans. But I'd dutifully read them, then tossed them in the trash. I didn't need progress reports to see how my apartment reconstruction was progressing. Not fast enough, is all I can say.

"We've both been busy since the wedding. With more important stuff." I waited to see if she'd rise to the challenge. Or not.

"Chloe and I had a nice time," she said. "I guess you and Sheli did, too."

"I haven't seen much of her lately." Pause. "I knew you were watching me." Okay, so I couldn't help myself. And I expected Megan to respond in kind.

Long pause. "I was gonna leave a note. About the painting."

I have to admit to a certain amount of disappointment, but decided that no reaction to my verbal challenge could mean we had a truce.

She gestured at the scrawled note on a yellow legal pad that lay at her feet. After a moment, she made room for me next to her on the stoop.

"What's that on your face?" I asked, tempted to touch her but determined to hold back.

She brushed at her cheeks, which only spread the white stuff.

Okay, so I gave in and tapped the tip of her nose. "Chalk?"

"Glaze."

I cocked a brow.

"I was painting," she explained.

"Isn't that what I'm paying the painters to do?"

"It's distressing."

"Sure is, if my interior designer has joined the crew."

"No. Distressing as in, a new painting technique," she explained. "For the kitchen cabinets."

"You're painting my natural maple kitchen cabinets."

"Just some sample boards. To see if it makes sense to make the cabinets look old."

"If you'd wanted old," I said, "maybe you should have kept the cabinets already there and saved a few dollars." I gazed upward. "Is it still too dangerous for me to go inside?"

A small smile curved her lips. "The female cabinet crew has left the building."

But obviously, from the distressed look still lingering in Megan's eyes, not everything was so okay out here. "I know we haven't been on the best terms lately," I said, "but if you wanna talk, I've got time to listen."

Megan took her time considering my simple question. I wished I knew what was going through her mind.

"Sure. I could use some advice." Pause. "But it's a personal problem. I hate to impose."

Uh-oh, I thought. Tread gently. If Megan's personal problem was me, she wouldn't be talking to me about it. "Isn't that what friends are for?"

She looked at me with a wistful expression on her face. And for a second there, I thought I'd stumped her.

"My old boss has underbid Design Time on two projects."

"That happens in any business."

"Projects they'd have turned up their noses at before."

"Before?"

"Before I left."

"Means you must be doing something right if they consider you competition."

"Or something wrong that's gonna lead me right into bankruptcy."

"What's your favorite color?"

Her jaw dropped. "This is how you help?"

"Humor me."

"Green," she said grudgingly.

"TV show?"

"How many points for saying *The D.A. Chronicles*?"

"Double points. Your favorite food?"

"Rita 2's potato salad. How do I get the secret recipe?"

"You don't. It's a secret."

Megan punched me hard. "That's not fair. I answered your questions."

"And I took your mind off your problem."

She leaned against my shoulder. It felt good. Right.

"Thanks. That bit of nonsense was just what I needed."

Just what I needed, too. For the first time since we'd had

sex, we were behaving like the best friends we'd once been. And if she wasn't going to quiz me on Sheli, then I didn't have to worry about answering.

Megan sighed. "Thanks for offering to help."

"No problem." Now all I needed to do was find the perfect time and place to implement The Code.

Which I still needed to memorize. Provided I could remember where I'd stashed it.

# 9

*Megan*

IN ONE OF MY WEAK(ER) moments on yet another dateless Friday night, I let Chloe talk me into speed dating.

"It will help take your mind off the situation with Jack." Chloe hit the DVD rewind button on the scene in *Sleepless in Seattle* where the heroine and her best friend cried over Cary Grant and Deborah Kerr in *An Affair to Remember*. As the disc played again, she said, "You won't regret the experience."

Easy for her to say. Chloe enjoyed the excitement of the chase. I was content, for now, to get my romance fix by watching Hollywood's take on how people stumbled through relationships.

As we watched the movie, and munched on popcorn and M&Ms, I finally told her what Jack had said about Sheli. "His exact words, 'I haven't seen much of her lately.'"

"Still, that doesn't mean he won't see much of her in the future," she said. "Or that if he totally stops seeing her, he'll see you. So you need to be proactive. Meet more men!"

The next night we boldly flagged a cab going downtown. Our destination, the Meat-Packing District.

We were dressed in our girly-girl clothes: sleeveless satin dresses (Chloe in peach, me in a deep purple that, surprisingly, didn't clash with my red hair), flowing silk printed shawls and shoes that made walking look impossible, if not impossibly hazardous to one's health.

Speed dating was Chloe's attempt (misguided) to locate Mr. Right Now. And how does that work?, you ask.

In Chloe's version of speed dating, you either get extremely lucky or go home, alone and depressed. You hit the party and/or club scene, pick a guy out of the hordes of horny men and let him wine you, dine you and attempt (not successfully) to get you into the sack. If you don't click, look for another guy. Next night, do it all over again. Then again. Until you find someone you can bear to wake up to and/or with the next morning.

Not that you actually have to sleep with him. You just have to *imagine* you could.

Personally, I found the entire concept of speed dating ridiculous as well as frightening, considering all the weirdos (of both sexes) trolling the streets. But this was what dating for singles in New York City had, sadly, become.

The taxi dropped us off at Fourteenth Street, just west of Ninth Avenue. Chloe had memorized a list of seven clubs (one for every night of the week, I guess) for us to check out.

"Pick one," she said.

I pulled two aspirin from the tiny fabric bag that hung around my waist, and sucked them down dry. I'm not a coward, but I didn't think I could handle anything like HunkMania tonight. Or ever. "How about Cooler?"

"Cool!" She nudged me in the direction of the front doors of what used to be a warehouse. Next door was a working warehouse (hence Meat-Packing District). Was that animal blood on the sidewalk? Or the walls? I didn't want to know. Really.

"There's a long line," I pointed out. A double line of stylish hims and hers, hims and hims and hers and hers snaked down the street and almost around the block.

"There's a long line for them," she responded. "And there's this for us." She held up a silver slice of plastic that resembled a credit card and shouted, Charter Member COOLER, under a facsimile of Chloe's face. Chloe flashed it (and a bright smile) at the tuxedo-clad bouncer who, I guess, was making sure that only cool people got into Cooler.

After examining the card, Chloe's face, and then the card again, he unhooked the satin rope and passed us through.

"Where did you get that?" I whispered.

"I was invited to apply." She riffled through her small beaded bag to reveal a set of plastic cards, one for every club in the Meat-Packing District.

I looked at Chloe with new respect. "You amaze me."

She shrugged. "Why live in New York City if you're not going to experience all its angles."

Despite my grave reservations about this outing, I was committed. Still, I couldn't disguise my immediate reaction as I hovered in the doorway—a wince from the too-loud noise.

Followed by a cringe, from spying too many people, most of them women who looked like us, although I prayed I didn't appear as desperate for:

a) a drink,
b) a fling, and/or
c) a bout of sex.

I prayed the aspirin kicked in fast, before the music pounded what was left of my mind into strained baby food.

Within moments, I met Bachelor Number One. Tad. Or

Ted. Or maybe Brad. He was tall, blond, dressed like all the guys at Cooler (in black) and wore a gold Rolex on his right wrist and a diamond stud in his left ear.

Since I couldn't really hear what he was saying, I just alternated nods with smiles. That seemed to work. At this point, I was worried I might do something uncool during my first few minutes in Cooler, embarrass Chloe (and all single women in the city) and get tossed out.

Therefore also putting a quick end to my term as a speed dater.

But I'd promised to give this a try, so...

My speed date nudged me away from the entrance, to a cozy little table for two whose current occupants (carbon copies of Tad/Ted/Brad) immediately melted into the crowd.

"Drink?" asked Tad/Ted/Brad.

I shook my head.

He seemed entirely too disappointed and, suddenly, I was less concerned about appearing uncool. My radar went on red alert: I knew about date rape drugs, about how scummy guys didn't hesitate to doctor their dates' drinks. Yet another reason not to blind date.

"I'm on the Street," he shouted across the table. "What's your biz?"

Oh, God, not another Wall Streeter. Trey had been my first. And my last. Please, please, please! Couldn't my first (and, the dating goddesses willing, last) speed date be with a normal guy? Minus the attitude and the earring.

Who was I kidding? Normal people didn't put themselves through this torture.

"I demolish personal property," I said, thinking how much fun it had been to take a sledgehammer and knock Jack's walls down. "And I'm really good at it."

That shut Tad/Ted/Brad up for a minute. I could tell by the confused expression on his perfectly chiseled face that he had no idea what I was talking about. Or if I was dangerous. But he was also trying to figure out a way he could make what I did pay off for him personally.

I tried to keep one eye on my speed date and another on Chloe, who was swallowed by the swelling crowd. I thought I spotted her on the postage stamp that passed for a dance floor.

"Dance?" I asked Tad/Ted/Brad.

He brightened. Maybe he figured if he couldn't get drugs down my throat he could get his hands on my body and still call the night a success.

You ever try to dance, let alone move, in an ocean of people? Especially when the person you were dancing with breathed so heavily into your ear that you could feel the spearmint from his mouthwash?

I loved to dance. I could go out dancing every night. With the right partner. Which this octopus dressed in a Wall Streeter's casual suit was not.

"Who are you thinking about?" Tad/Ted/Brad asked. Assuming, I guess, that the *who* would be him.

I was thinking about the last time I'd danced with Jack. Which had been at my engagement party. After two slow dances with me, Trey had gone off to chat with some friends of his father's and I'd tagged a reluctant Jack for the next fast dance. By the time I'd coaxed him onto the floor, the music had turned slow again. Then Trey cut in. Two beats later, Jack rapped Trey on the shoulder. Before the two of them could rearrange each other's faces, I shoved them both off the dance floor and tagged my oldest niece for the next fast dance.

Back to my speed date. Useless conversation followed. I mean, you've heard it all a thousand times before.

Him: Blah, Blah, Blah.

Me: How nice for you.

Him: Blah, Blah, Blah.

Me (thinking, You jerk!): How nice for you.

I found myself mentally comparing Tad/Ted/Brad with Jack.

Tad/Ted/Brad looked too good to be true. And probably was. Jack looked just good. Advantage, Jack.

Tad/Ted/Brad worked on Wall Street. Jack worked in TV. Advantage, Jack.

Tad/Ted/Brad liked to talk. About himself. Back when I was talking to Jack, he listened. Advantage, Jack.

After a few more minutes, I knew this experiment in speed dating was a total failure, and so I offered Tad/Ted/Brad my standard excuse:

"I just remembered. I forgot to change the cat litter before I left tonight. Gotta go. So nice to have met you."

My dance partner shifted right. I shifted left and moved along with the wave of people headed toward the bar. I found myself standing next to Chloe, who was sipping a Cosmopolitan and searching the crowd for other prospects.

Just so you know how I rated the evening, I conveniently forgot my pledge not to inhale liquor (for the second time in a month, the first being the leftover champagne from our women's encounter group) and took a small sip of Chloe's drink. I was tempted, for a crazy moment, to down the entire glass. "I can't believe people who meet at meet markets want to see each other in real life."

"You never know who you'll run into," she said. "Check out the area that's roped off. Private after-the-screening party. Don't look. Oh, look. Isn't that Brad Pitt? No. George Clooney? With J.Lo? No, he's got his arm around some hot model. This is so cool. What's the movie again?" she asked the bartender.

"*Stand Short, Live Tall,*" he said. "I've got a pivotal role. I'm the guy behind the bar who pours the drinks for Brad and George. You gotta hand it to TopNotch. They know how to throw an after-party."

TopNotch? Wasn't that the studio Sheli Bradshaw worked for? What if she was here? What if she had Jack with her? I casually scanned to the right, then left. No Sheli. No Jack.

Chloe was right. Just because Jack said he hadn't seen Sheli lately didn't mean he wouldn't see her again soon. What if again and soon were here and now? All I knew for certain was that I couldn't bear to see them together. Or hear that they'd been here. Definitely time to leave.

Chloe, on speed date number five tonight, decided to stay.

It was nearly one in the morning and raining pretty hard, but with the help of the club's bouncer I managed to flag a cab. Half an hour later, I snuggled in bed with my cat planted firmly on my toes and my eyes closed, but unable to fall sleep.

Every time I heard a noise outside, I imagined thousands of Tad/Ted/Brad clones lined up outside my building primed for continuous rounds of speed dating.

So I wasn't my sharpest when I boarded the train for Montclair the next morning. By ten, I was putting up wallpaper in the kids' bathroom at Patty's house.

My sister sat in the tub, arms curled around her knees, watching me very carefully. I guess she was waiting for me to break. Or something.

"You're too quiet," Patty said. "I don't like it."

"I'm all talked out." That was because I'd spent the train trip continuously talking on my cell phone with Patty, sharing my interpretations of the current state of Jack and Sheli's relationship along with my woeful tale of speed dating hell.

I yawned as I climbed up to the top of the three-step stepstool and dry fit the wallpaper. Then I climbed down slapped the back with glue, climbed back up and set it in place.

"Promise me you'll never speed date again."

I could do that. "But if I don't speed date, blind date or Internet date, what's left? I'm twenty-nine. The man I was going to marry didn't want to marry me. And his unique way of delivering the news might have left a permanent scar. One that other men, including the one who might someday want to marry me, will see. And then he'll know The Truth."

"I have no idea what you're talking about," Patty said. "But Trey's not the only man you can marry."

"You're keeping score?"

"What about Jack?"

"Ouch."

"C'mon, my asking that question can't hurt."

I held out my bloody finger. "I'm not bitching about what you asked. I'm bitching because I cut my finger with the razor blade when I heard what you asked."

"Listen, before you get all defensive."

"Hand me that last piece of border." I slathered on the glue, set the paper in place and smoothed out the bubbles.

"Excellent."

"You're just complimenting me now because you saved outrageous labor costs."

"Not true. But in addition to compliments, I'm offering valuable sisterly advice. Plus, I'll treat you to a large sausage and cheese pizza, extra cheese, for lunch."

"Go for it. I can't wait to hear how you came to the conclusion that Jack is a viable marriage option for me." I climbed down the stepstool, set it on the outside of the tub, and then sat down across from Patty, who'd scooted back enough to leave me room to flop. Everybody—from my psychic to Chloe and the women's group, and most especially the two Ritas—was eager to dish out advice. If I listened to them, why not listen to my sister?

"I think you're scared," Patty said. "But not because you won't find another man who will love you. You're scared because you are in love with Jack and you don't know what to do about him."

My brilliant sister had become delusional. Before I left Jersey today, I was going to toss out her romantic comedy DVDs and romance novels. "You think I'm in love with Jack?"

"I know you're in love with Jack. You've always loved him."

"Up until New Year's Eve, I loved him as a best friend. But I've never been romantically in love with him." Pause. "Yes, I am attracted to him. He's gorgeous and sexy, and what woman sucking in her last breath wouldn't be attracted. But attraction doesn't equal being in love. Don't look at me that way. I know what I'm talking about. I know what I feel. How I feel."

"Do you think about Jack all the time?"

"No." Yes.

"Do you want to be with him when you're not with him?"

"No." Yes.

"Megan, I can't help you if you're not honest with me. Or yourself."

Silence.

"Yes." Sigh. "Yes."

"That's better. Now, did you think about Trey all the time? Did you want to be with Trey when you weren't? *Be honest.*"

"No." Pause. "Aren't you going to ask me if sex with Trey was as good as sex with Jack?"

"I think you've already answered that."

"But sex with Jack changed everything."

"And you can't take back that intimacy. Or the feelings. So, either totally end the friendship or move it forward. Neither of you is happy. And it's making those of us who love you both, who want you both to be happy, absolutely totally miserable watching you guys fumble through this."

"Have you been talking to Vanessa?"

"Who's Vanessa?"

"My psychic."

"You went to a *psychic?*" Patty clapped her hands in delight. "Now this is way too cool. I've always wanted to do that. What did she say?"

"Which time?"

Patty's eyes widened. "You did visits? Tell me! I'm in awe of you."

And so I told her. About my sudden no-yes, yes-no tendencies, Jack as my destiny or downfall and Vanessa's voice mail message claiming that *it,* whatever that elusive *it* is, can't be the same but can be better. "I want to know why it can't be the same. And what if 'better' for Jack is Sheli Bradshaw?"

"You know she's not," Patty said. "Sheli is only relevant in Jack's life until he can wrap his XY chromosomes around the person he really wants—you."

"I know, she's a segue. Chloe explained it. But that doesn't mean he loves me."

"Do you think he's slept with her?"

"Chloe says no. When we saw them together, she was a cling-on." I shrugged. "So I don't think so."

"How many times have you replayed in your mind that night of sweaty sex with Jack, wishing it had ended differently, imagining ways that it had?"

"If my life with Jack were to go into TV syndication, that episode would run every night of the week."

"So, despite your qualms, it wasn't a horrible experience?"

"Great sex," I admitted.

"So why were you so upset with him that you walked out? Who knows what might have happened if you'd stayed? I think you were afraid if you told Jack how you felt, he wouldn't say he felt the same. Even if you weren't exactly sure how you felt."

Boy, she was good. "That's it in a nutshell."

"But deep down you know he cares for you. And that scares you. Because having sex changed your comfortable boy-girl friendship into an unpredictable man-woman sexual relationship. Which you can't control the way you controlled your friendship."

I knew that. Didn't I?

"So I sit Jack down, tell him what I thought I was feeling then, how I think I'm feeling now, and everything will be okay?"

"Are you crazy?" she asked. "That's the last thing you do."

Rewind here. "Let me get this straight. If I'd stayed and talked it out New Year's Day, I wouldn't be fretting about all this. But talking with Jack now about what happened would be mistake?"

"You got it."

No, I didn't. "You are nuts."

"Do you trust me?"

"Up until five minutes ago."

Patty stared at me. "Do you trust me?"

"Yes." Make that a reluctant yes.

"All right." She clapped her hands. "Now all we need is a plan."

"Let me make it clear for you," I told her. "As good as

being in love with Jack might be, I don't think it could ever be as good as our friendship. I think Vanessa was telling me that my friendship with Jack can't be the same, but it can be better. She said nothing about love." I *knew* I would have remembered if she did.

Patty started to argue, but then thought better of it. "Whatever you say. You know best."

Throughout the afternoon, into dinner and during cleanup, Patty quietly worked on her plan. After sending her husband, her children, our sister Ellyn and her family, my parents and the dogs off to the playground, Patty was ready to share.

"You need to spend quality time with him." Patty dragged me off to the kitchen where we loaded the dishwasher. "And what better place than in Jack's new home. How about getting him more involved in the project?"

I added the gel pack of detergent and turned on the dishwasher. "We're talking about Jack Spencer. The man who doesn't know a wrench from a pair of pliers. Recall, for a moment, the day he tried to put together Lisa's first bicycle."

Patty winced. "He even read the directions. Twice. Didn't Lisa finally figure it out for him?"

"Our year-old nephews could have put that bike together faster," I said. "Jack was just as hopeless at choosing his new kitchen cabinets. He closed his eyes, waved a finger and plopped it down onto the open catalog. If I hadn't intervened, he'd be looking forward to cohabitating with knotty pine. I don't want to think of him with a paintbrush in hand."

"Take him shopping." She settled into one of my mother's comfy kitchen chairs with a mug of coffee.

"Jack hates to shop." I poured my second cup of coffee, added lots of milk. "He used to bribe me to do it for him." Pause. "In a way, he's still bribing me. It's just costing him more."

"Forget about spending money. Do the time."

"Maybe I should audition for a role on *The D.A. Chronicles*," I joked.

"If that's what it takes," Patty said. "Your relationship has changed. Getting to know him all over again could be fun. I know you're up for the challenge. Go girl!"

I reminded myself during the train ride back to the city that Patty had promised me a plan, but not necessarily a plan that made sense. Or one that would work.

Meanwhile, Jack's renovation continued on schedule, and I had to find more work for Design Time.

The following Wednesday, I met with a cable TV talk show host, a woman who'd recently bought a tri-level brownstone apartment in Hell's Kitchen. The place needed tons of work, but the client had a hefty budget and was anxious to get started.

She'd read about me in that Sunday *Times* piece (you know, the one where I nicely dissed wedding planners). She hired me during our lunch at a trendy Forty-second Street café, based only on a few rough sketches I'd drawn on the butcher paper tablecloth (with crayons provided by management).

This unexpected networking was a godsend. Made losing those other two jobs (almost) bearable. What possibly sealed the deal was her reaction (a high five) to my reaction (applause) to her news flash that my old boss had tried to speed date her. And how she'd threatened to have the bouncer at Cooler toss him out of the club.

After lunch, she caught a cab uptown. I caught sight of Jack Spencer's face, larger-than-life, up on the marquee of the Little Shubert Theater across the street. It was matinee day, and in less than twenty minutes the curtain would rise on a preview performance of Jack's new play, *Out of Touch*.

I thought about what Patty had said—that I should find new common ground with Jack, spend more time with him to expand that common ground. Then we could be friends again.

And I was curious to see Jack's play, if only because he'd been uncharacteristically quiet about it. There wasn't time to run over to the half-price ticket booth on Times Square, so I handed the box office attendant my eternally tortured credit card. Seventy-five dollars later, I was led to my seat in the packed theater, about twenty rows from the stage.

Before I could check out the program, the theater lights dimmed and the curtain rose.

Jack's performance, in a word: funny.

And when the curtain fell, ending Act I, I stayed in my seat, thinking about that final scene. Which felt vaguely familiar.

Jack's character sprawled on the floor in front of a balance beam. "Won't you say 'I'm sorry'?'" he asked the woman he'd been unsuccessfully wooing since the moment the play began.

She smiled and replied, "I'm sorry you didn't fall harder on your ass."

(I remembered saying those exact words to Jack the night we teeter-tottered in Montclair.)

There was a knock and a second woman entered—a woman who was in real life Jack's acting buddy, Phoebe Silverstone, but who in costume and makeup reminded me of Sheli Bradshaw. She carried a long piece of paper, which trailed after her as she stalked the stage. She tossed Jack's character the paper and said, "There. Our life together. All plotted out. Just sign on the dotted line and I'll take care of everything."

(Not only did this character look like Sheli, talk and walk like Sheli, she had an obsession with lists like Sheli. Hmm.)

Another knock. A man entered, saw Jack on the floor, and smugly proclaimed to the first woman, "Aha! I'm not the only one sending you conflicting messages."

(Finally, one character I didn't recognize from my life. Wait, that character *could* be Trey.)

The first woman climbed on the balance beam. She walked across it without a wobble and announced, "I'm no longer listening to either of you."

(I said something vaguely similar to Trey and Jack during the dance portion of my engagement party.)

The other three exited, and Jack's character was alone on stage. He tried, but couldn't make it across the balance beam without falling. After several attempts, he gave up and asked, "Am I that out of touch?"

That question was answered in Act II. No spoiler here.

But I wanted to know more about the end of Act I.

I stayed in my seat during the final curtain call, and when the theater emptied, I wandered up to the box office.

"I'm a friend of Jack Spencer's," I told the woman behind the booth. "Any chance of leaving him a note?"

"Name?"

I told her.

"Let me see some ID."

I showed her my NY driver's license.

She pulled out a sheaf of clipped papers as thick as Manhattan's telephone book, shuffled through the pages, then glanced up at me in surprise. "Megan Sullivan. You're in here. You're cleared to go backstage."

She wasn't the only one surprised. But with pass in

hand, I followed her instructions to check with the head usher, who was busy counting and stacking playbills at the other end of the lobby. He readily agreed to take me up to see Jack. I trailed him through the empty theater, then up onto the stage, where the balance beam dominated the small space.

With a quick gaze to make sure no one was watching, I stepped onto the beam, made it across without a wobble (just like the female character in the play) and had to try it once more. Again, no wobble. I rushed to rejoin the usher, who told me, in all seriousness, "You might want to give the actors some lessons." Then he led me through a back-stage maze and up onto a rickety staircase, which was a lot more challenging than the balance beam.

When we got to the top, he pointed to the door at the end of the hall. "Door's usually open. If it's closed, knock."

Before I could knock, the door opened.

"Megan? *Megan!* What are you doing here?" Jack pulled me inside. He started cleaning up the small space, dumping everything (clothes, books, takeout cartons) off the love seat and onto the floor.

I sat on the love seat. Jack closed the door, leaned against it.

"Had lunch with a new client," I said. "Had some free time, so I thought I'd catch the matinee."

He looked at me warily. "We don't open 'til next week. It's gonna change a lot. I hope. What did you think?"

"I liked the play. Liked you." Pause. "Liked Sheli, too."

He cleared his throat. "Sam figured anyone who's met her and knows me, is gonna pick up on that. I'm doing what I can to keep her away."

"So you are still seeing her?"

"No. No, I'm not."

Long, awkward pause as we looked at each other.

"You seeing anyone?" he asked.

Time to see if Patty's advice might work. "No. No, I'm not."

Another long pause. Time to change the subject.

"*Biography* called. I'm up for the interview."

"Thanks. It will be nice to have a few friendly faces talking about me." He looked at me hopefully.

"The Ritas made a strong case."

"They fed you guilt with the potato salad."

"That, too. But I want to do it. The rest of America should know you the way I know you."

"That wail you hear isn't the air-conditioning wheezing to life, it's my ego taking a hit."

"I'm sorry. That came out wrong. I'm talking about Before."

"We can't go back, Megan."

"I *know* that." I fiddled with a loose thread on the love seat's slipcover.

"You never answered my question. Why are you here?"

"Why is my name on your 'okay to send backstage' list?"

"I'm an optimist."

This is what sped through my mind:

Chloe: *Speed date! Be proactive. Meet more men!*

Patty: *Getting to know Jack all over again could be fun.*

Vanessa: *It can't be the same. But it can be better.*

Speed dating versus spending time with, getting to know, the new and improved Jack Spencer. The prize: I'd get my best friend back.

The choice was obvious. I hoped I knew what I was doing.

# 10

*Jack*

MEGAN'S UNEXPECTED post-matinee visit totally inspired my performance that night.

Acting in a farce can be tricky because timing, on stage and off, is everything. Miss your cue or your mark, and it throws off the other actors. I hit my marks. And all my jokes. Even my numerous attempts to wobble across the balance beam (not an act) aroused heartier laughter and spontaneous applause.

If only people in real life were as easy to manipulate as theater audiences.

After weeks of often painful rehearsal, major rewrites from the playwright (sometimes delivered minutes before the curtain rose), undecipherable performance notes from our director and several previews where the audience sat in stunned silence at the end of Act II, I felt as though I'd finally "found" my character.

He was always going to be a bit clueless—hence, the title, *Out of Touch*—when it came to figuring out women. Unfortunately, men don't get a figuring-out-women gene at conception. I've been told that women get breasts and we get a compensation gene, one that's magnetized to attract women to us from the moment of our birth. The closer we get to puberty, the stronger our magnetic aura. If we're clever, we learn to manipulate this compensation gene in order to create an uneven playing field re: friendship and/or romance.

So, last night I finished memorizing The Code.

No way, despite warnings from Rachel and Alicia, was I gonna light a match to that five-by-seven-inch sheet of paper, aka My Future. Because as any actor learned, you never knew when you'd need to refer to the script.

Now I was prepared to implement The Code at the first opportunity. All I needed was a signal (clear preferred, hazy acceptable) that Megan would be receptive.

More good news. Over the past week, I've had a run of professional luck.

The play opened to rave reviews, and not one critic (or friend) had noticed, or mentioned, the remarkable similarities between my on-stage and off-stage lives.

Got a welcome call from my agent. The producers of *The D.A. Chronicles* had finally chosen which of the three endings to last season's cliff-hanger would open the new season. (They were, you may recall: Caitlin died, I died, we both died.)

A.D.A. Logan Hunter (me!) had survived the bullet to his back. Goodbye Caitlin, hello to new female character, who would be played by my current co-star, Phoebe Silverstone. Talk about karma. We would begin filming the new season the morning after our play closed next month.

Not that I'm superstitious, but I found not one, but two four-leaf clovers during an afternoon romp with Achilles in Riverside Park. Back at the apartment, I wrapped them in waxed paper and, recalling how the two Ritas used to save the maple and oak leaves Megan and I would bring home each fall, placed the two clovers between pages of

the heaviest book I could find. Actually, considering the
messy state of my apartment, the *only* book I could find—
the Manhattan telephone directory that was currently
doing double duty as a bedroom nightstand.

Luck continued with a v-mail from Sheli. She told me
she was decamping back to L.A. with the playwright of
*Out of Touch,* dumping both me and her job with TopNotch
Pictures.

If there was one surefire uncertainty in my life, it was
the *is-it-ever-going-to-end?* apartment renovation. What had
taken mere days to rip apart, back in early June, was going
to take months to put back together. It was only late July,
and I was living in a giant jigsaw puzzle with a few key
pieces (specifically, a working kitchen) missing.

Megan showed up at the apartment each morning
around eight, with a smile for everyone (including me) and
her project punch list. Once, when she was deep into consultation with the painting contractor, I sneaked a peek.

Her list was actually three columns: To Do, In Progress,
Done. (For the record, under Done, master suite including
bath; under In Progress, everything else. Under To Do, the
notation, Check In Progress.)

When I turned the paper over, I saw my name under-
lined and in capital letters with two exclamation points:
*JACK!!*

What followed detailed her expectations:

1) Keep Jack away from power tools, paint cans and/or
brushes, hammers and other items that could cause bodily harm to him or the construction crew. Or increase insurance coverage!

A wavy, black pencil line (had Megan changed her mind
or accomplished her mission?) ran through number one.

The next item, written in that same black pencil, led me

to believe it was a recent addition to the list, probably right after she'd scratched through number one.

2) Important! Jack's paying the bills. Keep him happy. Welcome his assistance. Give him light tasks to make him feel a part of the process.

As to light tasks, she meant such jobs as shuffling the apartment around, which is what we were doing today. The "we" being me and Sam Davies, whom I'd drafted to help.

Since eight that morning (Monday, my only day off), we'd been packing boxes with stuff from my old bedroom to move into my new master suite, so work could continue on this side of the apartment without disrupting my life (too) much. But now, at least, I had a huge bedroom (new furniture would be delivered in a few days), that walk-in closet with a window and a luxury bath with whirlpool tub, steam shower and his-and-her sinks.

Laughter echoed through the empty apartment and I followed the sound to the kitchen, which was still missing all of its major appliances. But the maple cabinets looked great. The walls had been painted white, mainly because I'd been holding off on making a decision on, as Chloe put it, a *real* color.

Earlier in the morning, Megan, Chloe and Sam had cast their votes for red, after telling me that the four of us would be painting that day. I remained undecided—on the color, and whether I was up for the painting job.

Sam held out the opened can of red paint. Bloodred, thank you very much. A little too red, if you wanted my honest opinion, which was obvious no one did because they'd chosen the color without me.

Megan offered a brush. "C'mon, Jack, live a little. Just one wall. It's not going to hurt."

"That's really red." Exaggerated sigh. "But you guys are

the professionals, I trust your judgment, so here goes." I hesitantly dipped the brush in the can and made a bold line down the wall.

We all stepped back to admire my work.

"Go for it," Sam advised.

"You can always repaint," Chloe offered diplomatically, "although I don't know why you would. This is gonna turn out terrific, especially if we add a little white glaze to soften the look."

I turned to Megan. "It's your kitchen, Jack," she said in all seriousness. "If you're really dead set against the red…"

"No," I said quickly. "I like it. It's just going to take some time to get used to."

That brought out a smile, one that almost made a red kitchen palatable. "That's the spirit. It takes courage to go red like this."

"Good move." Sam poured some paint into an aluminum painter's tray. I knew he wasn't talking just about my decision on the paint. He knew I was ready for The Code, had even quizzed me this morning, and I'd passed.

Megan handed both of us clean rollers. "I think you two he-men can handle this. Let us know when you're done. Chloe and I are gonna clean up the mess you guys made cleaning up the bedroom."

I nudged Sam. "Make yourself scarce so she has to work with me. Alone." I knew she would, because Megan the perfectionist wouldn't take a chance on letting me mess up her project. Even though, technically, it was my project.

Sam sputtered some lame excuse, handed Megan his roller and dragged a reluctant Chloe from the room. Achilles started barking. The front door slammed shut. Then the apartment was quiet. Good, they'd taken Achilles, leaving me and Megan alone.

"Guess you're stuck with me," I said cheerfully, as I rolled on a wide swath of red that reminded me of a Rorschach inkblot.

"The work will go faster," she said, expertly rolling on the paint. "Remember the last time we did this?"

I had to think about that. "No."

"We were six, maybe seven. We used our fingers."

Still didn't ring a memory bell.

"On this same kitchen wall," Megan prompted. "I can't believe you don't remember. It was a pivotal moment in our young lives."

The memory flooded back. One of us had been given an acrylic paint set, and we'd been left alone to allow our budding artistic creativity to flow. It didn't take us long to decide we needed a larger canvas than the one we'd been given. While our parents played cards in the dining room, we sneaked off to Rita 1's kitchen and left our primary-color handprints all over her newly painted white wall.

Needless to say, our parents were not amused.

End of painting indoors as a creative outlet for the two of us. Until now.

Okay, I couldn't help myself. I pressed my palm to a spot on the wet red wall, at the height I thought a seven-year-old could reach. "What do you think?"

Megan hunkered down and examined my artistic statement. "Needs something more." She planted her palm firmly on the wall next to my print. "There. Perfect."

We stepped back to examine our work.

And then, true to our childish natures, we added a few more handprints for good measure. When we'd finished, Megan waved her painted palms in front of my face.

"Don't use me as your paper towel," I warned. Too late. She pounced like a cat. I dodged, turned, but not quickly enough. Her palm slapped my back, and imprinted my favorite T-shirt (you know, the aqua Bad Boys one) in red.

I retaliated, of course. With a lunge.

Megan darted away, whipped a mean one-eighty. I grabbed for the back of her T-shirt, missed. I lunged again and wrapped my arms around her...breasts. Which, I will note here, were braless, and I felt her nipples harden.

"Not fair." She struggled, but not too much, although her bony elbow managed to solidly connect with my ribcage.

With my painted palms still planted you know where, I gave a tiny tug, and she fell back into my chest. "Forfeit?"

"When I'm winning? No way." She wiggled but I held on.

She stomped on my toe. All one hundred and twenty-plus pounds of her. Still, I didn't let go.

She went limp, like a rag doll, and that's when I almost lost my grip. Almost. As I started to prop her up, Megan's foot caught my ankle and we both went tumbling to the floor. Her reflexes were good, but mine were better.

She rolled and ended up on her back. I straddled her, keeping her arms above her head, wrists shackled by my hands. "Your strategy failed. Ready to cry 'uncle'?" I taunted.

Megan scowled. "You've never played fair."

"Excuse me." I let her feel just enough of my weight so she'd know who was in charge here. "We were playing nicely until you decided to finger paint on me."

"Couldn't help myself." She giggled. Then wiggled. And I got hard.

"Stop that giggling and wiggling." Of course, being Megan, she didn't. What she did do was try to flip me. And failed. We tussled, playfully at first. But then my hands found her breasts again. Her hands, now freed, found the snap on my jeans. And before either of us knew it we were breathing hard and heavy, my tongue tracing her nipples, her hands rubbing my penis, and then...

"We've. Got. To. Stop."

Guess which one of us panted out those words? If you guessed Megan, you are so wrong.

Those words popped out of my mouth. Because the last time we were going at it this hot and heavy—New Year's Eve on the rooftop of this building—I didn't exactly say stop, didn't want to stop, didn't stop. We'd had sex on that rooftop. Great sex. Great sex that had damaged our friendship almost beyond repair.

It had taken me more than half a year to get this close to Megan, to have her exactly where I wanted her, and I wasn't going to ruin it now by having sex with her.

Don't even try to search for logic in that statement.

Just know that I got up and gently tugged on Megan's arm, so that silently, but with both of us still breathing heavily, we could put ourselves back together. Without any assistance from each other. Although I was, you know, tempted, to help her. And I think Megan was tempted to help me.

"It was right to stop," she said, in a way that told me she was trying, really trying, to convince both of us. Then, from under her breath I heard, "There's gonna be a next time."

(Sure, she could have meant there's gonna be a next time and she's gonna get me first, but, optimist that I am...)

"That's a promise," I muttered. I ordered my mind to save and later print that little tussle, so I could remember just where we were when I'd played the hero.

Megan's fingers fluttered as she brushed them through her hair, telling me that our encounter had shaken her as it had shaken me. There was a moment of silence before she said, "It would be okay with me if you came out to Montclair for dinner next Sunday."

I let out the breath I'd been holding. "I can do that."

There wasn't time to say more because I heard the front door open, bringing home Achilles, Sam and Chloe.

So, following Sunday's matinee performance, I headed out to Montclair after picking up Achilles and a rental car.

It was nearly seven when I pulled in front of the Sullivan house and let Achilles loose to run up the drive and toward the backyard. Dinner was long over, but I knew there'd be a plate of leftovers left over for me.

I opened the back gate and saw assorted Sullivan family members scattered through the yard. My gaze shot to Megan, who was deep in conference with her sisters, Patty and Ellyn.

Achilles bounded across the deck, slobbered kisses over Megan's face, nestled his head on her lap and promptly went to sleep. Lucky dog. I wondered when I'd get a chance to do the same.

"Did my invitation get lost?" Patty asked slyly.

"Invitation to what?" I asked.

"Your personal painting party," Ellyn said. "Megan's been entertaining us with the details."

"Really?" I commented. "Did she tell you the part about me flipping her onto her ass?"

"No." Megan elbowed both of her sisters in their ribs. I saw them grimace, sympathized with their pain. "I did not."

"Can I?"

"Not if you value your personal assets."

And we both knew she wasn't referring to the stuff in the apartment. "Tell them whatever you want," I said graciously, "just as long as I don't read about it. Anywhere."

Jake, Megan's brother-in-law who owned a great antique store here in Montclair, motioned me over to the other side of the deck. He pulled a bottle of beer from the cooler and tossed it my way. "How's it going?"

"Define 'it,'" I countered.

He merely took a pull on his beer. "I hear the play's a hit. We've got tickets for Tuesday night. The apartment deconstruction is over and the reconstruction is under way. And…" He paused for effect.

I rolled my eyes. "Is everyone in this family obsessed with what's going on between me and Megan?"

"Well," Jake deadpanned, "you guys are making it so easy."

There was that.

I glanced over at the three women, heads together, locked in animated conversation and not paying any attention to Jake and me. Or so they wanted us to think.

"Any advice?" I asked. After all, he'd been with Patty for forever. They seemed as much in love as the day they married, more than ten years ago, and neither appeared battle-fatigued, although they juggled three great kids and two high-pressure jobs.

Jake was the kind of guy a guy could confide in and know that whatever you told him only went as far as his wife's ear, and that he, and she, were on your side.

Not that Sam Davies wasn't on my side. And not that I didn't value Sam's help. But Sam's point of view was, you had to admit, a bit skewed. And Phoebe? She'd already shown her true colors. She was on Megan's side.

The less said about Rachel and Alicia, the better, for now.

"Uh-uh." Jake glanced in the direction of his wife, who was now keeping one eye on us and the other on her children. "The three of them—" he was referring to the Sullivan sisters "—have been talking in code all afternoon. I've managed to decipher that Megan's made some major decision about you."

"What is this obsession women have with codes?"

"It's part of their genetic makeup. At least, that's what Patty tells me."

"Has she revealed The Code?"

Jake took a pull on his beer. "Are you kidding? A guy with The Code has unmatched power. Women give up The Code to guys, intentionally or not, they have to kill you."

Maybe it was better *not* to confide in Jake about what I knew.

"So you had sex," he continued. "Big deal. Have it again. And again."

Wait a minute. "Who told you Megan and I slept together?"

"Patty of course." Jake said. "But I'm sworn to secrecy."

"Obviously not."

"Don't worry," he advised. "Patty and I are in your corner. And Megan's. Who you guys choose to tell is your business—and only yours."

We joined the women on the other side of the deck.

"How's the renovation going?" Patty asked, her gaze lingering on me and then shifting pointedly to Megan. Considering Megan and I were now sitting at opposite ends of the large group (her with Achilles on the chaise, me on a deck chair), Patty had to raise her voice to get everyone's attention.

(I should mention here that Ellyn's husband, Tom, and Megan's parents contributed minimally to the conversation, but for the sake of brevity and staying on point I've left their comments out.)

"A few delays," Megan said with a shrug. "But that's to be expected considering how huge the project has grown."

(My translation: If Jack had moved out like I'd asked, we'd be weeks ahead and on budget.)

"You've got yourselves a challenging project," Patty said to me.

(My translation: Despite what might have happened during that painting party, she's not going to make it easy on you. Or: Forget about it. Or: Go for it. I was having some trouble reading her.)

"It will all be worth it in the end," Ellyn put in brightly. "Just think of all the new things Megan can spend Jack's money on."

(My translation: Don't muck it up. Or else.)

"Wait a minute." Patty snapped her fingers and everyone snapped to attention. "There's a lamp Jake found at an estate sale yesterday— You know, honey, the art deco one that I almost swiped for our bedroom. It's perfect for Jack. Megan, you have to see it."

"I'll come out early next Sunday," Megan said.

"The lamp will be gone by then," Patty said.

"I'll set it aside," Jake said.

"No," Patty said in as decisive a tone as I'd ever heard. "They have to see it tonight." To Jake, "Give Megan the key."

"I've got a free day tomorrow," I said, but was cut off by Patty's sharp, penetrating look that told me to get with the program or else.

"Megan has to work tomorrow," Ellyn put in quickly.

"If Jack has the day off and Megan's working for Jack…" Jake looked to Megan and me for confirmation.

Patty and Ellyn groaned.

Jake shook his head in defeat. "Fine. If you decide you want the lamp—" he handed Megan a silver key from his key chain "—just put it in my office. I'll write it up tomorrow."

Patty coughed.

"Yeah, yeah," Jake said. "I'll write it up with the usual family discount."

And so we were off to check out an antique art deco lamp that I had to have. And with a thirty percent family discount.

Megan grabbed her cell phone (which, I should note here, she's never without, and which is always on) and I grabbed Achilles. And we started to walk. I patted my back pocket. Time to decode The Code. Yeah, yeah. I know I was supposed to memorize and burn it, but what would I do if I forgot my lines?

Over the past week I'd kept asking myself: Was I desperate enough to entrust the future of my friendship with Megan to this Code—five somewhat inane "clues" that women used to interpret whether a man was really interested in them?

I wanted my best friend back. Okay, truth here, I wanted more, if I could swing it, so what did I have to lose? Other than (more) self-respect if Megan laughed in my face. It wouldn't be the first time. Only, I knew these stakes were higher.

When we reached the playground, I dug my cell phone from my pocket. As I finished punching out some numbers, Megan's cell phone, which she'd hooked onto her waist, rang.

She ignored it. The phone kept ringing. After ten rings, it stopped, and I hit redial. More ringing.

"Stop that!" She grabbed my phone.

"Aren't you going to answer it?" I grabbed back. "Could be an important call. One you don't want to miss."

"You are so weird. I know it's you." Pause at my look of skepticism. "My phone has a special 'Jack's calling' ring."

She was joking. Wasn't she? But that could explain why lately I've been bounced into her voice mail. So much for *When you're together, call her cell phone from your cell phone just to say hello.*

I pushed End Call. Megan's phone stopped ringing.

Achilles yanked on his leash, forcing Megan and me to

pick up our pace. "So, tell me, how is the renovation going?"

"Don't you *read* the reports I leave for you? Aren't you paying attention to what's going on in your own apartment? Don't you care that I'm quickly siphoning off your bank balance so I can retire in Rio?"

"Yes. Yes." Pause. "No."

*Ask questions, and then really listen to what she's saying* wasn't going too well. She had better questions.

It probably would be wiser to wait before trying *Gaze deep into her eyes during key moments in the conversation. Key moments will be evident.*

It didn't take us long to reach Cherry Street Antiques, which was located in the heart of what passed for Montclair's downtown.

Megan turned the key in the lock, opened the door and reached for the light switch.

My eyes were drawn immediately to the art deco lamp, less than a foot tall, and looking right at home on a mahogany end table that I imagined would look great next to my new chocolate leather sofa that I'd heard so much about but hadn't seen yet.

I didn't want to be greedy, but I wanted the table, too.

Megan examined the lamp close up then handed it to me for a look-see. "We'll take the table, too," she said.

She grabbed the lamp, I lifted the table, and we danced through the maze of unpacked boxes and rolls of bubble wrap that filled Jake's office.

Since Megan and I were alone, I figured there was no time like now to try out number three. Only Megan beat me to it.

As she gazed deeply into my eyes, I realized Megan had a lot more experience with this Code than I did.

"Have you been plotting with my sisters?" she asked.

"Of course not."

"Then explain."

"I don't know what you're talking about." I really didn't, and it didn't hurt that I sounded dazed and confused.

"Who gave you The Code?"

On the other hand...

"What's that supposed to mean?"

"How else do you explain why you're acting like some lovesick high school boy?"

"I am not."

"Jack, you're calling me on the cell when I'm practically standing next to you. What's next? You going to talk *to* me, not *at* me? And then look deep into my eyes until we're both dizzy?"

"I don't know what you're talking about." This time I tried for indignant. Hell, I was indignant. This Code wasn't translating the way Rachel and Alicia had promised. "Listen to yourself. Me plotting with your sisters. What's next? You gonna accuse the Ritas of being—" I hooked my fingers in the air to make quote marks "—'in on it'?" Pause. "Megan, you need to get a life."

"Classic Code overload." Megan shook her head sadly. "You are so out of touch with what women want."

"What if I said I was researching a role for a cable TV movie?"

"So that's why you've been reading those chick magazines?"

No time to stop and rewind now. We were on a roll. "I don't know what you want me to say. I want you back as my friend. I want to fix what's broken between us."

"Don't ask me to write your lines, Jack." Pause. Sigh. "One day we were friends. Then we had sex. The next day we weren't. Just saying you want to be friends, to fix things, isn't enough. We have to work at it."

"I'm not suggesting we should forget what happened," I said, "but that we should build on it."

"You make it sound so simple."

"Why can't it be?" I countered, determined to cut through all the female subtext, and trying hard not to let the fear I'd buried ooze to the surface. What if we couldn't be best friends, or any kind of friends, again? I knew enough to know we couldn't just "go back." There had to be...

I sucked in a deep breath. "What about grabbing for more? If...if that's what we both want."

"Is that what you want?" she asked.

"I don't know. But I do know we can't go on like this. Sniping at each other. Making everyone around us not want to be around us." I looked her in the eye. "We're good people. We need to start acting like good people again."

"I have to think about it." She scribbled a note for Jake and then walked out of the office, leaving me to wonder what to do next. Then she popped her head back in. "Are you coming?"

We started back home. In silence. When we stood in front of her parents' house, she said, "I've thought about it. I want to work together on fixing our relationship. Maybe we could...pre-date."

Pre-dating wasn't in The Code. It hadn't come up in my consultation with Rachel and Alicia. Or in any of the chick mags. "What the hell is a pre-date?"

"We spend time together. Doing things. Learning about each other. But it's not...exactly...dating." She waited a beat. "And then see where it all leads."

"So you're saying we're gonna work to reclaim our friendship and then see what's next." While she was taking her time to answer, I wondered if this was where I did number four: *When you drop her off at home, hug, don't kiss, her good-night.* Or should I just forget about The Code, and wing it?

"Yes." She straightened her shoulders. "It can't be the same. But it can be better."

"Okay." I had no idea what she was talking about. I hugged her. "Just remember to thank your sisters for giving us an excuse to talk this out."

"They inherited the lack-of-subtlety gene from my mother."

I started to follow her inside, but then remembered the final portion of The Code: *Look back over your shoulder as you walk away from her door.* I owed it to myself, and the men out there like me, to complete the mission. "I think Achilles still needs time out here."

And as I dragged the dog down the street, I glanced back to see Megan at the front door, watching me watching her. As I turned the corner, I looked back again. Megan was still there.

Maybe Rachel and Alicia knew what they were doing. Or maybe not.

Because when I got back to the Sullivans' house about ten minutes later, Megan was pacing the sidewalk. She looked up, saw me, and the expression on her face—relief mixed with worry—just about stopped my heart cold.

"Tell me," I demanded, wanting to know, yet not wanting to know.

"You need to get to Florida, Jack. Tonight. It's your father."

# 11

*Megan*

"HOW IS HE? WHERE IS HE? Who's with my mother?" Jack's questions poured out with the intensity of an erupting volcano.

My parents had strongly suggested I try to keep him calm. Since Jack had a don't-mess-with-me look in his eyes and the fact he outweighed me by at least seventy pounds—and, without a doubt, could steamroll right over me if he wanted to—this was going to be an impossible task.

"Your dad's in intensive care, but stable." I gently drew him into the house, keeping my fingers clamped on his arm (and making sure Achilles was safely inside) before closing the door. "The Ritas are on the phone now."

Jack slumped against the door and sucked in several deep breaths that brought natural color back to his face. "What happened?"

"He was hitting golf balls. Your mother saw him clutch his chest. The EMTs got there right away."

"That's it." Jack pulled out of my grasp and marched down the front hallway, toward the kitchen and the sound of my mother's soothing voice. "I'm moving them back to the city. Where they belong. Where I can keep my eye on them."

Jack had given two Oscar-worthy performances recently, the first when Rita 2 was diagnosed with breast cancer, and the second when his parents decided, after months of discussion, to move to Florida.

To me, however, Jack had confided all his fears. He'd wanted what was best for his mother, but was having a hard time accepting that his parents would be more than a thousand miles away, instead of a dozen subway stops uptown.

I sympathized. As much as I bitched about my Sunday forays into the jungle of Jersey, I couldn't imagine what it would be like not to have my family nearby.

Then, too, the Ritas had shared everything for more than thirty years, and in the back of my mind I'd wondered if they would share cancer as well. Rita 2's illness, and the stages of her recovery, were never far from my thoughts. And I didn't want to believe Jack's dad, or mine, was less than immortal. If a healthy Martin Spencer could get sick, so could the robust Patrick Sullivan. I'd grown up thinking of Jack's parents as my own, so all of the above gave me plenty to worry about.

"What do you want me to do?" I'd followed him to the kitchen, keeping my voice calm, which didn't seem to affect Jack's rising agitation.

So much for my skills as an empath.

"Get me on the next plane outta here." He handed me his platinum credit card, one whose escalating outstanding balance I was intimately familiar with. "I've got to talk to my mother."

Rita 1 wordlessly handed him the phone, then enveloped him in a big hug. I hovered at the doorway, wanting to stay with Jack, but she let go of him and quietly pulled me into the family room. I glanced out the bay window and saw my father playing with Achilles, and my sisters in quiet conversation on the back deck. My brothers-in-law had been dispatched to the city to pack Jack a bag for his unexpected trip.

"Go online," she told me. "Find Jack a flight."

"How bad?" I booted up the computer and tried to keep one ear tuned to the goings-on in the kitchen as I logged on to a travel website. Unfortunately, Jack wasn't projecting as loudly as he did on the stage, so I couldn't eavesdrop.

"Bad enough that she wants Jack with her tonight."

I checked the airline schedules from each of the three major metro New York airports. "He'd never make the last flight from Newark. Nothing more tonight from La-Guardia or JFK."

My mother hovered restlessly at my shoulder as I called up possible flights for the next morning. Looked like we were going to be making a before-dawn trip to the airport.

"You finish here," she said. "I'll let Jack know you've booked him a seat on the first flight from Newark."

Twenty minutes and about fifteen hundred dollars later, Jack had a round-trip, open-ended, totally refundable first-class aisle seat on the 7:25 a.m. flight to Fort Lauderdale.

Normally, I'm not so cavalier about spending large amounts of money, especially so much of someone else's money, unless they've hired me to do so. But I knew Jack would thank me later, especially since I'd saved him from an almost three-hour journey in coach, spent cramped in a center seat over the wing.

After carefully folding the printout of Jack's itinerary and receipt, I returned to the kitchen. He sat slumped in a chair, clutching the phone as a lifeline to his past, present and future.

"The doctor's in there now? Okay, I'll hang on. I'm not going anywhere. Not until tomorrow morning. You just tell me what the doctor says. Exactly what he says. Tell him I want to talk to Dad."

Jack got up, started pacing. "He plays golf," he muttered to no one in particular. "Thinks he's got the energy of Tiger Woods, and plays himself into a heart attack."

"You don't know for sure it's a heart attack," my mother soothed him. "Maybe it's just heatstroke."

"You think so?" Jack asked hopefully. "He's supposed to be busy retiring, enjoying himself, flirting with my mother. Not lying in a hospital bed, attached to monitors, wearing an oxygen mask…"

He clutched the phone to his ear. "Mom? Tell me what the doctor just said. Tell me Dad's heart is beating okay now."

After a moment, he handed me the phone and slid, like a mound of Jell-O, into the chair. "She says the doctor says he's gonna be fine. But that he can't talk on the phone now."

"Hi, Rita," I said in as cheerful a voice as I could muster. "It's Megan. No. *No*. Jack's fine. Concerned, but okay. He's just worried that you're… Yes. Of course. No problem. The doctor's still there? Good. Right. You go ahead. Don't worry about Jack. We'll…I'll…take care of him. And make sure he gets on the plane. I know. Yes." I brushed the tears from my eyes. "I love you both, too."

I passed the phone to my mother. "She says she can't hang up until she talks to you again."

Rita 1 pasted on her brightest smile (as if Rita 2 were comfortably seated across the kitchen table from her). She spoke to Jack's mother in a shorthand language known only to these two women. After a long silence, but a generous amount of nodding to whatever Rita 2 was saying, Mom ended the call.

"How sick can that man be if I can hear him arguing

with your mother," she told Jack. "You'll see for yourself once you get to Florida."

In the meantime, we—meaning I—had to help Jack through tonight.

"Get Jack and yourself settled in the guest room," my mom said softly. "I'll fill everyone in and then send them home. Your father needs his sleep if we're going to be at the airport by five-thirty."

Notice how smoothly she did that. Just assumed Jack and I would spend the night together, not engaged in sex, but because she knew he needed me and I needed to be there for him.

My constant analyzing of the whys and why nots, plus trying to make sense out of Vanessa the psychic's advice while listening to my heart, had shown me I could no more keep away from Jack Spencer than I could keep away from Spencer's Deli cherry (and, yes, blueberry) cheesecake. Nor did I want to.

But, as you know, timing (especially in love and romance) was everything, and tonight wasn't the right time, right place, or right night to dump my Big Revelation on Jack.

Jack dropped into bed fully clothed, and promptly fell asleep. He looked sexy enough to ravish. Vulnerable enough to cuddle up to. So I spent the long hours before dawn curled beside him, watching him, every once in a while making sure he was still breathing, and thinking about what to do.

About him. About us.

For far too long, I'd viewed Jack as my Big Mistake. Had doing so been a Big Mistake, too?

If there's one good thing I've learned over the past months, it's that any mistake, big or small, can be fixed. Re: my small mistake. Trey eloping with our wedding planner meant I'd avoided a likely split before we'd celebrated our first anniversary.

Re: Big Mistake, I wanted my best friend back. To accomplish this goal, I would need:

a) a well-thought-out plan that allowed for flexibility,
b) a certain willingness to admit I was wrong, and
c) extreme patience to deal with Jack's sure-to-be-an-earful reaction when I finally admitted I was wrong.

I didn't have a plan. Yet.

I'm working on admitting I was wrong. I know I've got a long way to go to fulfill my potential.

I am, and forever will be, impatient.

Cut to the next morning.

Shortly before dawn, I was planted (along with my parents, and Patty, who'd actually done the driving) in uncomfortable plastic chairs right in front of the main passenger security checkpoint at Newark Liberty International Airport, waiting for the first announcement that Jack's plane would begin boarding.

The battery on Jack's cell phone had died from overuse and undercharging, and for the past hour he'd used my cell to check in with Rita every fifteen minutes. He couldn't reach her now, which only added to his growing distress because the doctors still hadn't allowed him to talk directly to his father.

My mother finally wrestled the cell away from Jack and handed it to me. Without the phone to keep him occupied, Jack started to pace the length of the gate area.

"I need coffee." In mid-pace, Jack stopped, gazed around intently, then headed toward a kiosk that had just opened for breakfast.

My stomach growled. So did Patty's. We tried to look as pitiful as we could. Which wasn't that difficult. No one, other than Jack, it seemed, had gotten much sleep last night. Including Achilles, who'd spent the night with his head and front paws resting on my feet. As far as breakfast went, all we'd had time for was coffee.

My mother gave my father a pointed look. And so my father, who'd also been eyeing the kiosk filled with muffins and bagels with a hopeful look, happily trailed after Jack.

Mother settled back in her chair and closed her eyes.

On to other concerns I hadn't had a chance to voice last night. I quietly told Patty about Jack's weird behavior during our walk to and from the antique shop. "I want the truth," I said to her. "Did you slip him The Code?"

"No way." She paused. "My original idea was to get you to the store, tip the cops off to a possible break-in, and then maybe have you spend part of the night in jail together until we got around to bailing you out."

Only Jake threatening to withhold sex, Patty told me, had convinced her not to call the cops on us last night.

"Points for originality," I said. "And restraint."

"Thanks," Patty said modestly. "Wish I'd thought of The Code. I haven't had to use it in a long, long time. Actually, not since Jake proposed."

"Jack liked the deco lamp," I said. "That cool mahogany table, too."

"Knew he would. The renovation will be worthy of a spread in *House Beautiful*."

"You haven't seen it yet."

"I have faith in you," Patty replied with a smile and a wink.

I turned to my mother. "I'm going with Jack."

"Of course you are," she murmured, eyes still closed.

"Not for coffee. I'm going to Florida." I dug through my tiny handbag looking for my one and only credit card. I pulled it out and examined it carefully, wondering if the ticket agent would be able to tell just how badly I'd been treating it the past few weeks. "This is going to break my budget."

"You can't put a price tag on friendship." Those were my mother's words, but Patty said them.

"If I didn't love you all so much I'd never cross the Hudson River again. But don't," I warned my mother, "start counting grandchildren." I turned to my sister. "Or plan a wedding. I am merely supporting a friend."

Rita 1 and Patty shared a smile. And a wink, which they didn't think I saw. But I did. They made an optimistic pair.

Well, I guess I was into my plan. Part of which included my being there for Jack. Even if *there* turned out to be Fort Lauderdale during the hottest summer on record. And without a change of underwear or a fresh toothbrush.

I stood. "Better go buy that ticket."

As I headed toward the main ticketing area, I kept my eye out for Jack and my dad. But, true to the nature of men, they'd likely disappeared somewhere deep into the bowels of the airport, certain to surface thirty seconds before the plane took off, the two of them both fed and watered. And probably not carrying a cup of coffee or a bagel slathered in cream cheese between them for the rest of us.

The ticket counter was moderately busy, and as I stood in line, I prayed my credit card wouldn't melt on me. This flight wasn't going to be cheap, considering I was purchasing it about an hour before it left. We were talking close to a thousand bucks, even in coach. Shudder. But the peace of mind (mine) would be worth the cost.

Was I doing the right thing? *Yes,* my little voice told me.

How would Jack react when I boarded the plane with him? *He's gonna be relieved*, the voice said. *Don't worry*.

While I waited in line, I phoned Chloe, filled her in and told her that I'd be out of town just a couple of days.

"Matt Cochran has left you six voice mail messages since Friday afternoon," she told me. "Each sounded more petulant than the previous one." Pause. "He's offered you your old job back."

Matt was one of the senior partners at my old design firm, one of the trio of guys who'd predicted that if I went out on my own, I'd fall flat on my shapely you know what. He was also the man who'd introduced me to my ex-fiancé.

I didn't believe in holding grudges. Well, maybe just a little. "If he calls again, let it slip I've jetted to south Florida on a major design challenge."

Not far from the truth. And, if nothing else, that would have him panicking and sending one of his many over-worked assistants (of which I had been one) out for an aspirin haul.

And I'd tell Matt a big, "No, thank you," to his face once I got back to New York.

My next call caught my neighbor, who had my extra key, right before she left for work. She promised to check on the cat if I'd return the favor next month. No problem.

Ten minutes later, with all my personal business attended to, I was still standing near the end of the ticket line when I heard the first boarding call for the flight to Fort Lauderdale. Unless some major miracle occurred immediately, and the line in front of me magically disappeared, it was unlikely I'd be on that plane.

"I've been looking all over the damn airport for you," Jack growled into my ear as he hustled me out of line. "We're gonna miss the plane."

"I don't have a ticket."

"Then isn't it convenient I've got one for you? Right next to me in first class."

I started to protest, but Jack's hand covered my mouth. "Argue later. The ticket agent said the pilot's a fan of *The D.A. Chronicles*, but he's not gonna hold the plane forever."

"You know how I hate to fly." I tried not to whine, but it had suddenly occurred to me that if I got Jack to focus on my well-documented flying phobia, he wouldn't spend the next several hours fretting about his father. Not that he shouldn't or wouldn't worry, but there was nothing he could do until we got to Florida.

"Don't worry," he promised. "I'll hold your hand."

I'm happy to report, our flight was fairly uneventful. The complimentary breakfast with to-die-for coffee (real cream) and French toast (real maple syrup) was heavenly. Jack, who said he was too nervous to eat, eventually settled into his seat, his head on my lap, his eyes closed, his hand in mine and a big smile on his face.

Every time I shut my eyes, the plane hit an air pocket, so for the next three hours I watched Jack. Which could easily become a habit.

Our touchdown in Fort Lauderdale was right on time, and with a bump so slight I wouldn't have noticed it if I hadn't been staring out the window, watching the ground rush to meet us.

Jack grabbed his carry-on from the overhead bin, and, after he signed autographs for the entire flight crew, we dashed through the concourse, down an escalator that seemed to go on forever, and to a well-known rental car agency.

The young woman at the counter, perky and not a day over eighteen, greeted Jack like a long-lost friend. "You're here!" she squealed, and came around the counter to give him a hug.

To me she said, "Take our picture."

Then to Jack, "The minute I saw your reservation come across the computer this morning, I bought one of those disposable cameras. Now everyone will believe that I really met Logan Hunter."

I did the camera thing and waited until Jack, who'd barely been able to get a word in edgewise and who I could tell was anxious to get to the hospital but reluctant to disappoint a fan, could pull himself way.

Several dozen photo ops later (all the car rental agents and the baggage claim workers seemed to be fans of Jack's show), Jack picked up the keys to a spiffy red convertible. Within minutes, we were flying along Interstate 95 at close to eighty miles per hour, a speed rarely accomplished in metro New York.

While the fan scene at the car rental booth closely resembled the one during our unfortunate lunch at my favorite Italian restaurant, I mentally reviewed what had happened at Giorgio's—and with the crew on the plane—with a clearer vision. All those people felt Jack belonged to them because they spent an hour a week watching him as Logan Hunter, a character in a TV drama. But I knew the real Jack Spencer, a man who could make me laugh and cry while frustrating me to the point of wanting to bash him over the head with one of the two-by-fours from the renovation, which, so far, I'd managed to keep from doing.

What I didn't know, however, was what to expect when we arrived at the hospital. So it was reassuring to see Jack's dad sitting up in bed, intently watching the Golf Channel on a TV mounted from the ceiling, while Rita 2 kept both eyes on him.

I hovered in the doorway while father and son bonded.

Rita 2 motioned me over. She wrapped me in a bony hug and then stood back to gaze at me, a stern look fixed on her face. She lightly pinched my cheeks. "Megan didn't let a little thing like her fear of flying stop her from coming to see you," she told Jack's dad. "What other fears will she conquer today?"

You've heard this before, but it bears repeating: Subtlety, thy name is *not* Rita.

I peered around Rita 2's shoulder to see Jack's dad wink at me. "Don't I get a hug?" He extended his arms wide.

"You scared us," I whispered as I fell into his embrace.

"A little indigestion, that's all," he said. "Rita worries too much."

"Retirement isn't supposed to land you in the hospital," Jack said.

Over the next half hour, the two of them bantered back and forth, talking about Spencer's Delis, whether the Yankees would win the American League Championship and the World Series, the reviews of Jack's play that he'd sent them and the upcoming filming of their portion of Jack's TV biography.

All in all, a typical afternoon at home chatting with the Spencers, if one didn't take into account the unusual location, that being a hospital room.

I was wiped. Rita 2 was, too.

"Your mom needs some rest," I told Jack. "Stay with your dad. I'll drive her home."

He handed me the keys. "The condo's a few miles away. Come back in about two hours?"

"Sure," I said. After fifteen minutes of goodbyes, another ten to get to the condo, a promise that I'd eat—because, according to Rita 2, "You're too thin, Megan. Eat some potato salad. There's fresh made in the fridge."—I finally had Rita 2 settled on the back deck with a cup of tea and her favorite daytime drama on the battery-powered TV.

I took a quick tour of the condo—two bedrooms, each with a bath, a great room with vaulted ceilings and a large eat-in kitchen. While the condo lacked the architectural details that had made the Manhattan co-op unique, I had to give Rita 2 credit for decorating tastefully—and a couple of extra points for not dragging the seventies to Florida with her, except for the queen-size water bed in the guest room. I wondered what Jack would say about that.

The laundry room was conveniently located next to the guest bath, so after I dropped Jack's duffel onto the floor, I stripped off my clothes and tossed them into the washer and myself into the whirlpool tub, where for the next twenty-seven minutes (the wash cycle), I proceeded to soak away. That done, I rustled through Jack's stuff, searching for something to wear while my clothes rolled around in the dryer.

Aha! The guys had packed Jack's Caution! Bad Boy At Work T-shirt, freshly laundered but still carrying a somewhat faded paint imprint of my palm. I shrugged into it, and a pair of Jack's boxers, then curled up under one of my mother's handmade quilts made especially for Rita 2 and closed my eyes, figuring Jack's mother would let me know when to collect Jack.

Sigh. Peace at last. I could hear the ocean. The call of the gulls. Feel the slight breeze, that smelled like rain, blowing through my hair. Wait a minute. What was I doing in the middle of the ocean, sleeping on the wing of a plane that was bobbing up and down?

Cautiously, I opened my eyes to see Jack sitting on the

edge of the undulating water bed, his eyes covered by a new pair of sunglasses—the kind where he could see out and all I could see was me.

He lowered the glasses onto the tip of his nose and peered down at me.

"Good. You're still breathing," he said.

"Get out," I grumbled, pulling on the quilt. "I assume you spent the past two hours quizzing the doctor. What did he say?"

"Dad didn't have a heart attack, but something like a heart bump. Mixed with some heat exhaustion." Jack's eyes widened as I sat up and the quilt slipped. "You're sleeping in my T-shirt. I want it back. What else you got on underneath there?"

"Go away. I'm going to tell Rita 2 you're harassing me."

"You won't." He gently yanked on the quilt. "Are you naked under there?" He ripped the quilt out of my hand, and off the bed, with a flourish, revealing the boxer shorts.

"You do those tiny heart shapes proud." He grinned.

"You're not going to seduce me."

"Wouldn't try." Pause. Followed by a wicked grin. "Wanna seduce me?"

"No way." In a heartbeat.

I tried to keep my voice steady. After all, I sat in the middle of a water bed dressed in, well, actually undressed, except for Jack's T-shirt and boxers.

He cocked a brow. "If you're feeling a bit shy about getting naked, you can model for me instead."

"I'll pass," I said dryly.

But talk about fast moves. Before I knew it, he'd straddled me. "Tell me what you want."

"A million bucks, after taxes." What I really wanted was

to get wet and naked with Jack. I longed for him to touch me, to taste me. When he did, I felt my heart race, my breath catch.

He chuckled as he brushed his lips against my forehead. I saw the little nick where the razor had grazed his chin this morning, when we'd shared the bathroom. Before I could kiss the hurt away, Jack's finger traced a line from the sensitive spot in the middle of my forehead, down the tip of my nose, to the little shallow dent in my chin. When his finger caught on the rim of the T-shirt—actually, his T-shirt—he pulled at it until it showed the start of my cleavage.

Jack kissed my breasts through the tee, and a thrill of desire ran through my body. Before I lost all rational thought, I gulped in a deep breath, only to have Jack kiss my breasts again. Both of us watched my nipples react. Then he hardened.

As I reached out to touch him, I was thinking, okay, our body parts now are in sync. Last New Year's Eve, our body parts were in sync, but we weren't actually thinking. Well I'm thinking now. Five minutes ago I'd wanted Jack as my best friend. Now I wanted more, even if I wasn't exactly sure what "more" meant or what "more" was.

But I was reasonably sure "more" meant more than lust, more than a quickie, more than the crumbled relationship we ended up with after we'd slept together last New Year's Eve.

Then it hit me. This wasn't the same. It was better. Because I loved Jack Spencer. No, it was better than that. I was in love with Jack. Talk about emotional overload. "I...lo..."

"What did you say?" Jack asked.

I tried to suck in some much-needed air. "We need to talk."

"Don't tell me how after pre-dating, we spend the next

few months talking before we actually have a date." He
sighed. "Or land in bed again."

"Yes, please." I smiled.

Jack's green eyes bored into mine. "You want to talk?
Now?"

I could almost see his mind at work:

*Heated kisses = male ecstasy. Talk = cold shower.*

Finally, he said, "Answer this. Does sex follow talking?"

I was starting to enjoy myself. I liked being in love with
Jack. He was handsome, witty and sexy, and because I
knew him so well, I didn't have to worry that he'd ever
blindside me. "I expect there will be physical gratification."

"I can buy that." Pause. Jack looked at me strangely, as
though he'd never seen me before. "Let's get married."

"You are so not funny." I punched him in the gut. I
didn't want to think about weddings and that kind of stuff.
I was just getting used to thinking about being in love
with him. "The last time someone proposed, he ran off
with our wedding planner." Pause. "And we both know
how that chapter of my life ended."

"It's not supposed to be funny. It's a marriage proposal."

Guess I was wrong about being blindsided.

"I asked you to marry me," he said almost too quietly.

"I don't know what to say."

"Say yes."

"I can't…I don't… How can I trust…*love?*" Thoughts
were crowding my mind so fast I couldn't process them.
And what came out didn't make any sense.

"What's all that supposed to mean?" He got off me and
sat on the edge of the bed, close enough that I could see
the hurt mixed with the anger on his face. "You can't because some jerk who didn't deserve you in the first place
dumped you at the altar? You won't because you had great

sex with me and then, like a coward, walked out? You can't because you won't trust me enough to know I'd never leave you?"

Talk about a one-two-three punch. The force of his words, more than the words themselves, knocked me further off balance. My mouth moved frantically as if I were a fish out of water as I tried to take back everything I'd said but didn't mean, to tell him I loved him. But nothing came out.

"Megan." Jack reached for me and I jerked back. "I'm sorry. I didn't mean any of that."

I took a deep breath, trying to regain my equilibrium. After all we'd been through together, we always returned to what had happened *after* we'd had sex. "Don't say you're sorry, Jack, for speaking what you believe is the truth. I really have to go…be somewhere else, anywhere else. By myself."

"Trey left you Megan. I'm not Trey. Know what I think? It's *you*, you don't know. *You*, you don't trust."

I slid out of bed, fussed at the dryer and put on my clean clothes, all the while keeping my back to Jack. I couldn't look him in the eye, afraid of what I'd see. Or what he'd see in me.

"You can't keep walking out on me, Megan," he said in the coldest tone I'd ever heard, "and expect me to be there when it's convenient for you."

He brushed past me without a backward glance. The front door slammed, and I winced at the sound of squealing tires as Jack drove off. This time he'd left me. I knew he wouldn't be back soon.

Rita 2 couldn't help but hear all the commotion we'd made, and she fussed around the kitchen, trying to put a positive spin on everything, while I called a taxi to take me to the airport. I had to go home.

All I could think about on the flight back to Newark was that my Big Mistake hadn't been having sex with Jack last New Year's Eve, it was how having sex had changed the way I saw myself in relation to him. Because I'd always believed our being friends meant we shouldn't, and couldn't, be lovers, too. And thought Jack had felt the same.

And then I'd fallen in love with him.

But was Jack right? That not only did I not have enough faith in him, I didn't have enough faith in me.

If so, chalk up another Big Mistake.

# 12

*Jack*

AS FAR AS EXIT LINES went, I'd like to think mine deserved a standing ovation.

Megan responded by scurrying back to New York.

My mother took a less-than-subtle approach. When I returned to the condo, she shoved a plastic spoon and a pint of freshly made potato salad at me and told me to go to my room and not show my face again until I had a foolproof plan to (legally) give her grandchildren.

Behind closed doors at the scene of my "crime," and over spoonfuls of potato salad, I contemplated my less-than-successful proposal. I'd never asked a woman to marry me (except in *Out of Touch*, and the final curtain fell on Act II before I got an answer). So I'd expected that when I did, the woman I asked would say yes. Not run away.

I hadn't planned on proposing to Megan at that moment. The words spilled out, but once I'd said them, I knew I meant them. I wanted—no needed—to be married to Megan. And have her married to me.

Because I'd loved Megan Sullivan long before New Year's Eve. Now I was *in love* with her. She made me laugh, made me cry, drove me nuts, but, hey, I loved all that, too.

She was, and would always be, my best friend. Maybe we'd had to survive this anomaly in our friendship, and all our not-so-serious relationships with other people (i.e., Trey, the jerk who broke Megan's heart, and the Jekyll-Hyde Sheli), until it was our time.

Which was supposed to be now.

But Megan had said no, and I'd reacted just the way you'd expect any guy so rudely rejected to respond—with oral combat.

I'd tossed back a few truths I knew she wasn't prepared to hear. Stuff I thought I needed to say right then. Considering the outcome, maybe I was wrong. Maybe.

I had no problem identifying my big mistakes, but I was less confident about how to fix them. Especially when the person I wanted to fix things with was determined to pretend I didn't exist.

On the flight back home, I told myself I'd give her enough time, and space, to come to her senses. By the time I'd landed, I'd run out of patience.

Achilles was happy to see me when I picked him up at the Sullivans'. The Sullivans were happy to see me, too. Rita 1 told me I'd just missed the *Biography* TV crew, the interview had gone well and she'd had my mother on the speakerphone so she could listen in. I'd totally forgotten that today was the day.

My dog was anxious to get home. I was, too. Achilles spent the entire drive back to the city trying to climb into the front seat and onto my lap.

By the time we reached the apartment, I was exhausted, while my dog brimmed over with energy. He raced up the stairs. I slumped in the elevator with just enough strength to press the button. But I promised myself I'd call Megan the next day (without a foolproof plan, or even a plan a fool could follow).

But she beat me to it.

I'd barely grabbed Achilles from the stairway and gotten the apartment door open when the phone rang.

"'Lo," I said, as I struggled to untangle myself from duffel, dog and leash.

"It's Megan." Pause. "I didn't expect you'd be there. I was going to leave a message."

"I'm here. Talk. But unless you've changed your mind, we don't have much to chat about."

"I know you're upset with me, Jack, and I deserve your anger. I've got a lot to think about. We both do. Maybe it would be best if Chloe finished overseeing the renovation. It's practically done. Just needs a few finishing touches over the next couple of weeks."

"Are you suggesting, or telling me?" I held my breath.

A slight hesitation before, "Telling you. That was going to be my message." '

Exhaled. "It doesn't have to end this way."

"Tell that to Vanessa." Click.

Vanessa? Who the hell was Vanessa? Why did that name sound familiar?

An update since that conversation:

My father's still playing golf, but now on the Game Boy I bought him, and in full view of my mother.

I was back at work on *The D.A. Chronicles*.

Neither Rachel nor Alicia was speaking to me (Sam tattled how I'd blown The Code, and they took it as a personal affront).

Phoebe Silverstone, my new co-star on the show, shook her head sadly whenever she saw me. She offered to fix me up, once, and after I declined she hasn't offered again.

Chloe Farrell, Megan's business partner, stepped in to finish overseeing the work on the apartment. Which took more than a few weeks. Each time Chloe came over, she announced she didn't want to get in the middle of whatever was going on between me and Megan.

Whenever I spoke to the Ritas, they were careful not to mention Megan. (Was it their ploy to get me to ask questions, their acceptance that the friendship was definitely over, or their hope I was still working on a plan?)

I'd lost my appetite for cheesecake. And my mother's potato salad. This was not good.

Five months from that day in late May (when Megan had shoved her way back into my life), I wrote the end to the apartment renovation.

Less than an hour ago, Chloe had come by for a final walk-through, and now I was ready to start life post-Megan Sullivan.

Because I was done. Totally over her. Wiped her off the slate of my life. No way would she invade my mind or my space.

Although every time I looked around my new place, I saw Megan's touches and influences. The green walls. The chocolate leather couch and sink-into-me red leather chair. The mission-style coffee table. The art deco lamp and funky mahogany end table from Jake's antique shop. The two wood-burning fireplaces turned into one after a spirited discussion that Megan had fought and won.

But, I told myself, that feeling would pass as I continued to put bits and pieces of me into my new home. My sanctuary.

Oh, who was I kidding? I wasn't over Megan. I was miserable. And rumor had it (Chloe finally told much after I promised to fix her up with an actor friend) that Megan was miserable, too.

And I'd figured out who Vanessa was, because Megan's sister, Patty, had let it slip—the psychic with the storefront down in Chelsea. Only Megan Sullivan would trust her future to a psychic. But, then again, look what I'd trusted my future to—chick magazines and an undecipherable code.

I was as guilty as Megan for the sorry state our relationship had found itself in. Neither of us had trusted the other. Or ourselves.

Only Sam Davies seemed to understand my feelings. Or so I thought.

I'd invited Sam over for pizza and beer, along with a first look at my remodeled apartment and a preview of the rough cut of my TV biography, scheduled to air in a few weeks. The producer had included a brief note listing family, friends and colleagues who'd been interviewed. The list included Megan.

But before Sam and I got down to the pleasure of watching my life story reduced to fifty or so minutes (plus commercials), I was taking care of old business. I lit a fire in the fireplace and tossed in the paper containing you know what. "Should have torched this Code before I'd read it," I called out to Sam.

"Hmm," was all I heard (along with the clinking of beer bottles) from my twenty-first-century stainless steel kitchen that I wondered if I'd ever use. Then, "Hey, Jack, what are you going to do about this wall?"

"What wall?"

"The red kitchen wall with the handprints."

Oh, *that* wall.

"I get painter's block whenever I lug the can of touch-up out of the closet." I'd tried to get up the courage to make those handprints disappear forever. But I couldn't.

Was this another sign I was (foolishly) holding on to my past? I posed this question to Sam.

"Yes," Sam said, as he bit into a huge slice of pizza that

dripped with melted cheese and thick sauce. "The only answer is for you to sell the apartment to someone who can appreciate your angst. And these cool color choices. Someone like me."

I waved the *Biography* tape in front of him. "It's just a rough cut. There's still time to delete you."

Sam shrugged and took a pull on his beer. "Some of my best scenes will live forever on the cutting-room floor. I'll survive." Pause. "But will you?"

I popped the tape into the DVD/VCR combo, and hit Play. "You think I should call her and grovel my way back into her good graces, even though I'm the wronged one here. That I should put my ego on the line and tell her I can't live without her. And then sit back and let her reject me again."

"Doesn't matter what I think, Jack. It's what you think. What you do. And while you're reflecting on what you did, didn't or might do, did it ever occur to you that adding *I love you* to your marriage edict might have given you the answer you wanted?"

"I wouldn't have asked Megan to marry me if I didn't love her." And yes, I know I didn't exactly answer Sam's question. I *wanted* to remember that I'd told her I loved her—in fact, I know someone said "love," but it's a toss-up on whether that somebody was me.

I picked up the remote and fast-forwarded about halfway through the program, until I got to Megan's interview. I settled into my new red leather chair, my dog at my feet, bottle of beer on the table and piece of pizza in hand.

They'd filmed Megan on the back deck of her parents' home just a few weeks ago. The leaves on the trees had started to turn from the shade of Megan's eyes to the brilliant reddish-gold of her hair.

Megan was sitting on the chaise lounge and saying something about us growing up together. What was it that Megan had in her lap? Nah, couldn't be. I glanced over at the fireplace mantel. My silver-framed baby photo was not where it belonged.

An image from our first meeting to discuss the apartment renovation flashed through my mind. I felt my heart stop, then drop to the floor.

"Well, well," Sam said with enough admiration in his voice to flood Manhattan. "Is that you? Naked? Lookin' good."

"What the hell was she thinking?" I grabbed the remote and hit Stop in mid-scene.

"Forget searching for subtext," Sam said. "She's talking loud and clear." He took the remote out of my hand, hit Rewind and let that scene play again. I hit the stop button on the machine right at the introduction of the baby photo. He whistled. "Way to go, Megan! Sing it out!"

"She's gone too far." I struggled with my feelings as I struggled into my leather bomber jacket. Since the latter was the usual signal to Achilles that we were going for a walk, he brought me his leash. "You can't come with me. No witnesses."

"Take him," Sam advised. He popped the tape out of the VCR. "And take this. Present her with evidence of her treachery."

"Right," I growled, stuffing the tape into my pocket, then shoving the dog out the door and down the stairs.

By the time we got down to the moonlit street, I was madder than mad. How could she do that to me on a program that would air on national TV? I hailed a cab, followed Achilles inside and gave the driver Megan's address.

Traffic cruised smoothly down Seventh Avenue until we got to the beginnings of Greenwich Village, where there is no rhyme or reason to the street layout. After a few wrong turns, the taxi pulled up in front of Megan's place on Minetta Lane.

I looked up at her window. The lights were on. She'd better be home. I trailed a group of people into the building, left them at the elevator and climbed the stairs to Megan's second-floor apartment. Before I could pound on her door and demand an explanation, the door opened.

"I've been expecting you." She glanced down at Achilles. "And you."

I stood in the doorway, totally confused. Quick, someone, read me my lines.

"Sam called," she said.

"Then you know why I'm here." I waved the videocassette in her face. And made a mental note to deal with Sam Davies later.

"If you don't come in and close the door," Megan said, as she disappeared into her closet of a kitchen, "all my neighbors will know, too."

I nudged the door shut and shrugged out of my jacket, which I tossed on a coat rack decorated with purses, scarves and jewelry. "You don't look too upset for someone who knows she's made a big mistake."

"It won't be the first time," Megan said dryly. "Or, considering our history, the last. Sam said you saw the video."

"Up to the part when you waved that naked baby photo in front of the camera."

She rolled her eyes and took the video. She popped it in her VCR and shoved me onto her couch, then offered me the remote and Achilles some treats. "Watch it all," she advised gravely. "I'll be on the balcony."

I looked down at Achilles, who was gnawing contentedly on some beef jerky, then glanced over to the open French doors where Megan stood bathed in the moonlight. "Why do I know I'm not going to like this?" I muttered.

I hit Rewind, and then fast-forwarded to the beginning of Megan's performance. Nothing had changed since my last viewing. Megan sat on the chaise, holding that us-naked-together-as-toddlers photo and saying...

Listen for yourself:

"When I was younger," Megan told the invisible interviewer, "I considered Jack a bratty brother. When he turned thirteen, I saw him for what he really was—a teenage hormone. I waited until I was sixteen, and then I let him kiss me. We've been best friends since forever."

Accurate, but she could have spoken with more passion.

"Five words to describe Jack Spencer?" (Why was she using a full minute of camera time to think?) "Loyal," she finally said. "Persistent. Sexy. Funny. I need six words. Very stubborn."

She offered an impish smile (one that didn't fool me). "Don't believe everything you read in the gossip rags about Jack. But I will share one little secret..."

It was at this point that she actually held up the naked baby photo and the camera zoomed in on my privacy. And here was where I'd stopped watching. But now I let the video run.

"Well, I know Jack will get all embarrassed, but he is the first man I got naked with." The video Megan looked me directly in the eye. "And, I hope, the last. I have faith that when he sees this interview, he'll understand what I'm talking about."

I hit Stop. And turned to see Megan in the doorway.

"What am I supposed to understand?"

"You're going to make me say it?"

"Damn straight. According to you, I'm not just stubborn, I'm very stubborn." I waited for her to say something. She didn't. "You know I can't make this easy for you. Because, if I did, you'd never let me forget it."

"You are so competitive."

"You wouldn't have me any other way."

"True." She straightened her shoulders. "I'm sorry…"

"Sorry that you're going to embarrass me on national TV?"

"Only in that other women get to see you naked."

"C'mon, Megan, out with it. If you're gonna tease more than a million TV viewers, you can tell me what you were trying to say. Give me a break. I've been working without a net here since New Year's."

She took a few steps toward me. "I do love you, Jack. And I'm in love with you. But I thought New Year's Eve was about pity sex. I was so embarrassed. That's what sent me running."

"It was never about pity sex," I said.

"I know that now. I'm sorry I let my insecurities get in the way of our friendship. Sorry I thought having sex would change everything between us. It did, of course, but I made a mess out of it. Because I didn't realize until it was almost too late, and was afraid to admit to myself that what we had was special." Megan took a deep breath. "I'm sorry I didn't trust you. Or trust myself. I know it doesn't make sense, but I was so afraid that if we fell in love, we'd fall out of our friendship." She hesitated. "I have to ask you something."

"Yes," I said immediately.

"You haven't heard the question."

"Doesn't matter. I trust you. I've been in love with you

forever. I'm sorry—no, I'm thankful—you didn't find what you were looking for with Trey. I'm not sorry about what we did last New Year's Eve. I love you. I'm only sorry it's taken me this long to tell you what I wanted to tell you then." Pause. "You know that part in the wedding ceremony when the minister asks, 'If anyone has a reason why this couple shouldn't be married…'?"

Megan stepped back and sagged against the French doors. "You wouldn't have!"

"I'd been rehearsing my lines for days," I said. "So, you see, there's nothing you can ask of me that I won't say yes to."

She narrowed her gaze. "Nothing?"

"If it's doable," I said modestly, "I'll deliver."

"That includes Rita 2's secret recipe for potato salad?"

I winced. "Ah, Megan, I said 'doable.' You know there's only one way you're getting that recipe—you have to marry me."

Megan laughed. "I do."

# Epilogue

*Megan*

SINGLE LIFE LESSON #2: If you're lucky enough to survive a Big Mistake, don't give up until you turn him into your Best Mistake.

Today was my lucky day. It was New Year's Eve, cold enough for it to snow and stick, and the flakes were quickly collecting in piles around me and on me. I perched on the steps outside of Jack's apartment on Riverside Drive, waiting for man and dog to return from their walk in the park.

I had big plans for tonight. Along with a few surprises.

(Hints: rooftop, champagne, get naked. I was determined to continue the New Year's Eve tradition we'd begun last year.)

I don't want to leave you with the impression that life with Jack cruised smoothly along after we'd admitted our mistakes back in October. As you've witnessed, Jack and I tend to be very stubborn and very impulsive, and although we think we know each other very well, we're learning how to deal with new things—and new things about each other—every day. Stuff like:

a) Achilles loves cats, but my Maine coon so far refuses to be friends. And after one unfortunate incident (an emergency trip to the vet, where Achilles needed six stitches on his nose), we've decided to let the two of them work out their relationship by themselves. It may take longer, but—unlike our friends and family, and especially the two Ritas—we've decided it's wiser never to meddle.

b) Just when you think an apartment renovation is complete, you find new things you'd wished you'd done differently. (Forget Jack's superstrong coffee in the morning, the red kitchen wall is its own wake-up call. The color goes, soon, but the handprints stay no matter what...)

c) Being in love (with Jack) is pretty much like being best friends (with Jack), only better. Vanessa the psychic was right, and we owe her big-time.

I heard a bark, and Achilles dashed down the street toward me, finally skidding to a stop at my feet. Jack followed, a bit out of breath, and nudged me over so he could sit.

"What's that?" he pointed to the cream vellum envelope.

"It's from Vanessa." I gave Jack the envelope.

He looked at it skeptically before opening it. "You know what's inside."

I nodded.

A moment later he passed it to me. "How the hell does she know these things?"

Dear Megan and Jack,
The first day of spring is the perfect time for a wedding. Don't worry about the crazy NYC weather. I predict the snow will stop by then.

"She's astute enough to know that when I said no, I meant yes," I said. "When I told her you were making me crazy, she knew exactly who I was talking about. Then announced that you were my destiny or my downfall. So it makes total sense to me she'd know the date we'd chosen to get married." I looked at the postmark on the envelope. "Almost a week before we did."

Jack wrapped an arm around my shoulders. "Do you think she has any idea what we're going to do next? Besides being buried in the snow if we continue to sit here."

"Not unless she's channeling us," I said between shivers. "But I predict when the ball falls in Times Square eleven minutes from now, officially declaring last year out and the new year in, we'll say 'I love you,' kiss each other senseless and get naked on the rooftop."

"Are you ready?" Jack asked solemnly.

I led him up the front steps and into the brownstone, with Achilles trailing behind us.

Jack punched the elevator button as the dog bounded up the stairs. We looked at each other, grinned, then raced up after the dog. Jack shoved Achilles into the apartment and then chased me up to the roof where we proceeded to…

(Hint: the answer is, all of the above.)

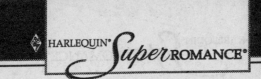

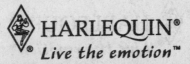

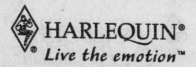

# Harlequin Romance®

Every month, sample the fresh new talent in
Harlequin Romance®!
For sparkling, emotional, feel-good romance, try:

January 2005
## Marriage Make-Over, #3830
by *Ally Blake*

February 2005
## Hired by Mr. Right, #3834
by *Nicola Marsh*

March 2005
## For Our Children's Sake, #3838
by *Natasha Oakley*

April 2005
## The Bridal Bet, #3842
by *Trish Wylie*

*The shining new stars of tomorrow!*

*Available wherever Harlequin books are sold.*

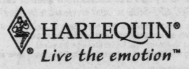

HARLEQUIN®
*Live the emotion*™

If you enjoyed what you just read,
then we've got an offer you can't resist!

# Take 2 bestselling
# love stories FREE!

# Plus get a FREE surprise gift!